The Story of Gold and Silver

This edition published 2025
by Living Book Press

ISBN: 978-1-76153-535-2 (hardcover)

978-1-76153-548-2 (softcover)

First published in 1920.

This edition is based on the 1920 printing by The Penn Publishing Company.

A catalogue record for this book is available from the National Library of Australia

The Story of Gold and Silver

by

Elizabeth I. Samuel

OTHER BOOKS IN THIS SERIES AVAILABLE FROM LIVING BOOK PRESS

The Story of Glass
The Story of Leather
The Story of Silk
The Story of Sugar
The Story of Porcelain
The Story of Lumber
The Story of Wool
The Story of Cotton
The Story of Iron
The Story of Gold and Silver

PLEASE NOTE

These books were written about 100 years ago and show the way people talked, thought, and acted back then. They tell the story of how resources like cotton, lumber, leather, and gold were developed—a process that depended on the hard work of many people. Sometimes the work was done by those who made the profits, and other times it was done by people who were not free, including enslaved individuals.

We know that some parts of these stories include ideas that we now understand to be hurtful and unfair. Our aim in republishing these books is not to support those old views but to share our history so we can all learn from it. By looking at the past, including its mistakes, we hope to learn important lessons that will help us create a kinder and fairer future.

We invite you to read these stories with an awareness of their time and to think about how far we have come—and how much work there is still to do.

Contents

CHAPTER I

THE GOLDEN STATE

PLACERVILLE, Placerville!" shouted the big brakeman at one end of the car; and hardly had he stopped, before the little brakeman at the other end seemed to echo the words, as he, too, shouted, "Placerville, Placerville!"

"Here we are at last," said Mr. Stanton, taking down his own suitcase, and then the two small suitcases that belonged to his sons Richard and Henry. Richard was so nearly thirteen that he was beginning to feel very much older than Henry, who was, as his father said, "only half-past ten." The boys were very glad to be in California, because their grandmother had told them many stories about her brother Dick, who had gone to California when she was only a girl. Now that they were in the very country where he had been, they were so eager to see everything about them, that they quite forgot that their father had told them that they must learn to look after their own things.

"Where is that umbrella of yours, Henry?" asked his father.

"I thought it was here, father, but it isn't," answered Henry, looking in the corner of the seat.

"When you've been in California a little longer, you will learn that it doesn't rain here in the summer as it does in New York, so we shan't have to keep such close track of that umbrella," said his father.

"Here it is," said Richard, pulling it out from under the next seat, just as the train reached the station.

"Run ahead, boys, while I count to see whether we have everything: two boys; two suitcases; one umbrella. Yes, we are all here."

"Carriage, sir, carriage!" called a man, coming up to them, as soon as they were fairly off the train.

"Can you take us to the place where Sutter's Mill used to be?" asked Mr. Stanton.

"This way, sir, right this way!"

The carriage proved to be only a two-seated open wagon, and the horse looked as if he could not travel very fast; but the country about them was so beautiful in its summer dress, that Mr. Stanton, and the boys, too, did not mind going slowly.

"Did Uncle Dick live in Placerville, father?" asked Richard.

"I don't know where he did live, when he first came out to California," answered his father, "if you call it living; for, in those days, they had only tents and blankets. I don't suppose there was a house here in '49."

"Did you say '49, sir?" said the driver, turning to look at Mr. Stanton, who sat on the back seat with Henry.

"Yes; my mother's brother came out here in the gold rush of '49."

"And found that nugget of gold father has on his watch chain," said Richard.

"Guess you've never been in the gold region before, young man," said the driver, looking down at Richard. "That isn't just the kind of gold they found here."

"Uncle Dick told me that he found this in a mine," said Mr. Stanton. "The '49 gold was placer gold, little scales or grains of gold, wasn't it?"

"Yes, sir. When they find gold in gravel or in the bottom of a river, they call it placer gold."

"Father," asked Richard, "how could gold get into the bottom of a river?"

"You see that we are at the foot of the Sierra Nevada Mountains, don't you?"

"Yes, father."

"Well, then, the rain and the melting snow got into the cracks in the rocks, and washed out some of the gold; and, when the water froze in the cracks, it broke off pieces of the rock, for water expands when it freezes—you remember how that pitcher broke last winter, when you left it out on the window sill with some water in it?"

"Yes, father."

"Then the brooks brought the gold down to the river. That sort of thing had been going on for a good many years, before the miners came. That's the way, isn't it, driver?"

"Yes, sir. And the gold is so much heavier than the gravel and sand that it sinks to the bottom, and stays there. That's the kind of gold they found here in '49."

"Did they dig the gold up with a shovel, father?" asked Henry.

"Yes, they did; but they got a lot of sand with it; and then they washed the sand out in pans and cradles."

"Cradles, father; what do you mean?" asked Richard.

"I'm right about the cradles, am I not, driver?" asked Mr. Stanton.

"That's what they called them, sir. At first the 'forty-niners' had only common pans, to wash the gold in; but, after a while, they put boxes on rockers, and put pieces of blankets in the boxes, before they put the sand in. Then they put the sand in, and one man rocked the cradle, while the other man poured on the water. Had to keep the cradle moving, too, sir; didn't do to stop."

"What was the blanket for?" asked Richard.

"To catch the fine gold, young man. They picked out the coarse gold, then they washed the blanket and got the fine gold."

"Listen to that, Richard," said his father, leaning over the seat. "Didn't one of your Christmas books have something in it about the Greeks that went over into Asia to find the 'Golden Fleece'?"

"Yes, father, but that was a sheepskin made of gold."

"Hardly, my son," said his father, smiling. "It was probably a sheepskin that they used to catch the gold in, just as the miners here used the blanket. I'm inclined to think Jason and his men rushed for the gold that had been found in Colchis, in much the same way that the 'forty-niners' rushed to California. I wonder whether you know who was the richest man in those old times?"

"Croesus, father; I know that!" said Henry.

"Right! And when you read Homer, you'll learn about the river Pactolus, where he got his gold. His gold was placer gold."

"So was the gold they found in Alaska, sir," said the driver.

"And in Australia, too," added Mr. Stanton. "Gold draws men to distant parts of the world where they would never think of going for anything else; and, when they get to the new places, they soon make towns and cities."

"But the first men have a hard time, sir," said the driver.

"Men that open up a new country always have a hard time," said Mr. Stanton. "They deserve much more honor than they generally receive, for they are really heroes of progress."

Richard liked to hear about heroes, for he wanted, more than anything else, to be a hero. So, turning to his father, he asked:

"How could they be heroes? Didn't they just dig gold and work in mines?"

"I rather think, my son," answered his father, "that the kind of heroes that came out here, would be a better kind to imitate than most of the heroes that you read about. The men that work in mines have to be brave all the time; and they have to be unselfish, for they often have to think of other people first."

Richard didn't say anything more, for he remembered, just then, a good many things that his father had said to him about learning to be unselfish.

"I can hardly believe, driver," said Mr. Stanton, "that, only sixty years ago there was nothing but a fort at Sacramento."

"Just Sutter's Fort, sir. He and his men certainly had a hard time, for they didn't have much to eat; and, when their clothes wore out, they had to shoot antelopes to get the skins for clothes. Couldn't tell a white man from an Indian, till you got up to him."

"Indians!" exclaimed Henry.

"Yes, young man; you wait till I've changed drivers, and I'll tell you about them."

"Who is going to drive?" asked Richard.

"I thought perhaps you would," answered the driver, with a twinkle in his eye.

"Truly?" said Richard.

"Sure," said the driver, handing him the reins. "I want a chance to turn around and tell this brother of yours about the Indians. Besides, I never did like to drive up hill."

"Grandfather lets me drive sometimes," said Richard, without taking his eyes off the horse.

"I thought you handled the ribbons as if you had held them before," answered the driver, turning half around in his seat, and winking at Mr. Stanton.

"Were the Indians real Indians?" asked Henry.

"Real Indians, my boy, dressed in deerskin; and when they dressed up, they wore feathers on their heads."

"Tomahawks, too?"

"They had bows and arrows, but I never heard of their having tomahawks. They weren't so fierce as some Indians; besides, the Spanish missionaries had been here a great many years, and they had made them good Indians. There were Indians all over California when the Spanish came; and there were more Indians than anything else when Sutter came. I don't suppose you know enough about history to know who discovered California, do you?"

"Yes," answered Henry, "I do. I heard a man at the mission tell mother that the Spaniards did."

"Here," said the driver, taking a long flat billbook from his inside coat pocket, "is a picture that I cut out of an old book. It's Sutter's Mill in 1848."

"I'm very glad to see this," said Mr. Stanton, taking the print. "Only a house, some sheds and the mill."

"And a United States Flag," said Henry.

"That flag must have meant a good deal to them. Hadn't been flying here long," said the driver. "Rather handsomer than the Bear Flag."

"The Bear Flag!" exclaimed Henry. "What kind of a bear?"

"One thing at a time, Henry," said his father. "I should like to hear about the flag. I know that Spain turned California over to Mexico, so the second flag must have been a Mexican flag. Did the Bear Flag come next?"

"Yes, sir. The white settlers wanted to be free, so they took Sutter's Fort, and pulled down the Mexican Flag. Then one of the men took some white cotton cloth, and painted a bear on it, with some charcoal and grease, and ran it up on the flag pole."

"Were there any real bears around?" asked Henry.

"Regular grizzlies, young man, plenty of them; some of them weighed as much as a horse. The settlers had pretty lively times with the grizzlies."

"Wasn't there a Bear Flag War?" asked Mr. Stanton.

"That's what they called it, sir. Don't think there was much bloodshed, for the Mexicans didn't care to have much fighting with the settlers and Indians. Marshall, the man that found the gold, fought in the Bear Flag War; then he went back to the fort to work for Sutter."

"Where did Marshall come from, in the first place?" asked Mr. Stanton.

"From New Jersey; but he came here on horseback from Missouri."

"Please, driver," said Richard, "there's a team coming, and I don't believe I can turn out. It's pretty narrow here."

"Just pull on the right rein, young man; Tom will understand, and do the rest."

Richard pulled hard on the rein. Somehow the horse found room enough and they drove safely past.

"That was well done," said the driver. "If you would like to have me, I'll take the reins now. I notice that we haven't heard from you for some time. Perhaps you would like to have a chance to talk, now that this brother of yours has asked all that he wants to about bears and Indians."

"Thank you, driver," said Richard, giving him the reins. "I think, when you're driving a horse; you have to keep your mind on it."

"You do, at any rate, till you and your horse get as well acquainted as Tom and I are. We understand each other pretty well, now, don't we, Tommy?" said the driver, touching Tom with the whip.

"Father," asked Richard, turning around, "did Uncle Dick come out on horseback?"

"No, he came in a ship around Cape Horn. He went to sea when he was a boy."

"Did most of the miners come on horseback?"

"No," answered the driver, "they came in wagons drawn

by oxen. The 'Merchants' Express' had twenty thousand yoke of oxen to freight across the country."

"Did they bring letters, too?" asked Mr. Stanton.

"Letters came by the 'Pony Express.' What do you suppose, young man," said the driver to Richard, "they used to charge to bring a letter from New York?"

"Fifty cents!"

"Guess again."

"One dollar!"

"Two dollars!" called Henry from the back seat.

"You guess, too, father," said Richard.

"I know," said Mr. Stanton, "for I found an old letter that Uncle Dick wrote grandma. He said that it cost five dollars."

"Five dollars!" exclaimed both the boys at once.

"And what do you think of a man that could ride almost four hundred miles, without stopping for anything but to get something to eat and to change horses?"

"I don't see how he could," said Richard.

"But 'Pony Bob' could do it, and did it," said the driver, with a flourish of his whip. "Did it, too, in just about a day and a half."

"I think," said Mr. Stanton, "that the men of those days were not afraid of work. I'm glad they were willing to ride so fast and so far, for letters must have meant a great deal both to the miners and to their friends at home. Aren't we almost at the place where the gold was found?"

"Yes," answered the driver, "in a few minutes we shall come to the statue of Marshall."

CHAPTER II

THE MAN WHO FOUND THE GOLD

I'VE brought a good many people out here," said the driver, turning toward Mr. Stanton, as if he thought it was time for him to find out something more about his passengers, "but I never brought any boys before. I don't see but they are almost as much interested in the trip as you are."

"I had to come West, just now, on business for my firm in New York, and I'm having a vacation, too," said Mr. Stanton, "so I brought the whole family with me. Mrs. Stanton and our little daughter, Edith, are in Sacramento. I'm hoping the journey will teach the boys to see things when they look at them."

"How funny that sounds, father!" said Henry. " Don't people always see things when they look at them?"

"The kind of seeing that I mean," answered his father," means knowing something about a thing after you have looked at it. I expect that you boys are going to learn a great deal from what you see this summer. That's why I brought you along."

"I see the statue!" exclaimed Henry, pointing ahead, as they turned a corner.

"Yes," said the driver. "That is Marshall, the man that found gold at Sutter's Mill in '48. Down there by the river is where the mill used to be."

"So this is really the man!" said Mr. Stanton, when the driver stopped in front of the big, bronze statue. "I feel like taking off my hat to him, and to the river that started twenty thousand men on a rush for gold in '48."

"Must have been pretty exciting for Marshall, that day when he found the gold," said the driver. "He walked forty miles to tell Sutter about it; and then Sutter hardly believed him."

"Did you ever see Marshall, driver?"

"I saw him once, when I was a boy, and heard him tell about his finding gold."

"I wish you would tell the boys the story."

"You see, Marshall came up the river to find a place for a sawmill to furnish lumber for Sutter down at his fort. Marshall was a wagon-builder by trade, so he made a good carpenter, when he got here.

"He looked a long time, before he found this place; but this suited him, and he got some Indians and a few white men to help him build a mill.

"When they tried to start the wheel, it stuck in the sand, and wouldn't turn round. Then they went to work to dig a deeper place. They dug in the daytime, and turned the water on at night, so as to wash out as much sand as they could.

Every morning Marshall went to look at the millrace; and, one morning, he saw something yellow, down in the water. When he got it out, it was a piece of gold, half the size of a pea."

"Did he know that it was gold?" asked Mr. Stanton.

"He thought it might be gold, but he wasn't sure. He pounded it, and it didn't break, so that made him pretty sure. After that he found a lot of small pieces, dust they call it; and then he went back to the fort, and he and Sutter tested it with nitric acid. That was the way the thing began, sir."

"How could he test it with acid?" asked Richard.

"That's one way that they test gold," answered the driver. "You see, nitric acid will dissolve a good many things, but it doesn't affect the gold at all."

"Didn't the Indians know that there was gold here?" asked Mr. Stanton.

"Yes, sir. When Marshall showed them the gold, they told him that their ancestors knew all about it; but that it belonged to a demon who ate up everybody that tried to get it."

"I can hardly wonder at the story," said Mr. Stanton. "So many men have died in the search for gold, that the Indians might easily believe that they had been devoured by a demon. But we mustn't stay here any longer; for, if we don't hurry, we shall miss our train."

"We haven't any post cards, father," said Richard.

"That's so. Seems to me I see some over in that window. Hurry as fast as you can!"

In a few minutes, the boys came back, and climbed into the wagon.

"See, father," said Henry, "here is a card almost like the

picture the driver showed us; and here is one of that pretty house on the hill over there, all covered with vines."

"And here is one," said Richard, "of the place where the river comes out of the mountains. See how high the rocks are on both sides! I never saw anything like that before. It isn't a bit like our rivers at home."

"We haven't any such mountains as these," said his father. "The banks of the Sierra rivers are very high, almost as if the rocks of the mountains had opened to make a place for the rivers to run in. Some of the canyons, as they call them, are hundreds of feet deep. The trees here are very beautiful, aren't they? Just look at that grove of pines, over on the slope."

"Father," said Richard, after they had ridden some distance in silence, "did all those miners that you talked about get rich?"

"No, my son; they were rich one day, and poor the next. They had to pay so much for food and clothing, that they had little left in the end. Uncle Dick told me that he once paid thirty-six dollars for a pair of boots."

"I don't doubt that," said the driver. "It was hard work to get anything to wear. The miners used to patch their clothes with old flour sacks. It took most of what they earned to keep them in food. Marshall himself died poor."

"After all," said Mr. Stanton, "gold isn't worth much, if you don't have a chance to buy what you need with it. But, even if they didn't make much money, they did a good work; for they opened up a beautiful country, so their work wasn't lost."

"How about you?" asked the driver, turning to Henry. "Any more questions about bears and Indians?"

"No," answered Henry, "but I should like to see a bear. I've seen several Indians."

"I have one more question," said Mr. Stanton. "May I ask whether you were ever in the mines yourself?"

"Yes, sir. When I was young, I worked in the Comstock—that was where the silver rush began, you know, sir. After a while they struck gold—lots of it. Those were great days, sir; but I gave up mining, because I like to be out of doors, not underground. If you want to see mining, sir, you'd better go over there."

"I am going there next week," said Mr. Stanton. "I've heard a good deal about the Comstock."

"May we go, too?" asked Richard and Henry, almost in the same breath.

"What!" said their father, "are you youngsters going to turn prospectors? We shall have to talk that over with mother. Just now we must make that train for Sacramento."

CHAPTER III

ACROSS THE SNOWY MOUNTAINS

NOW, boys," said their father, a week later, when they were on their way to Nevada, "what do you think gold prospectors do?"

"They bore down into the ground until they find the gold," answered Henry.

"Sometimes they bore into the side of a mountain," said Richard.

"Right, so far; but the next question is, how do they know where to bore? Suppose we began to bore anywhere, what should we find first?"

"Dirt," said Henry.

"The men that bored grandfather's well found water," said Richard.

"Then, if we bored and bored and bored, what should we find?"

"Rocks," said Henry.

"We should get down to 'bedrock,' as the miners say," his father went on; "but, if we could go down deep, as some of the mines do, it would grow warm, and the water down there would be hot; and, if we could go way, way down, the geologists tell us that we should come to hot melted rock."

"Our teacher told us that when we studied about volcanoes, in the geography," said Richard.

"That's right," said his father, "and the hot springs that are sometimes found, tell us the same kind of story, so we know that the center of the earth is hot; and we call the outside of the earth the crust of the earth.

"Long, long ago, the whole earth was hot, like the sun. When it began to cool, and the crust was thin, it shrank up and made ridges and hollows, 'like the skin of a dried-up apple.'"

"Then that's where the mountains came from," said Richard.

"That's the way they began; and then there were earthquakes, and the melted rocks that had gold and silver in them, were forced up into the cracks, and the gold and silver stayed there.

"Sometimes the water that had minerals in it came up to the surface, and then the water dried up and left the gold behind. And volcanoes, too, helped to give us gold, for some of the best mines, today, are in what seem to be the craters of old volcanoes."

"Is there gold in water, father?"

"Yes, Henry, there is gold in the sea, now; and men have tried to get the gold from the sea. Perhaps the chemists will be able to do it some day. If it weren't for the chemists, we shouldn't be able to get gold out of the rocks, for many rocks have only a little gold in them. Getting gold, now, isn't so easy as it was when Uncle Dick came to California. When we reach Nevada, we shall find men working down in the earth."

"Dick, what are you watching?" asked Henry.

"I'm watching the mountains. See, father, aren't they grand? They're all pointed at the top, and some of them are covered with snow."

"Yes, there's always snow on some of them. The Spanish called them sierras, because they look like the teeth of a saw."

While the boys and their father were watching the mountains, a young man opposite them, who had been smiling in a friendly way, as he now and then caught Henry's eye, left his seat and went to the end of the car.

When he came back, he lifted his hat and said:

"I'm Bailey, prospector. Wouldn't you like to go with me to the rear of the car, where you can get a look at the mountains?"

"Thank you," answered Mr. Stanton; "I should like to, if they will allow us to do so."

"I have been over this road so many times that they give me certain privileges," said the young man, turning to lead the way.

Stepping out on the platform, they found that the train was beginning to climb the mountain; and they saw, as they reached a curve, the chain of pointed mountains rising up from the beautiful valley below.

Henry, standing a little behind the rest, held his father's hand close; but Richard stood with both hands on the brake, and did not seem to hear his father, when he said: "I think we had better go back into the car."

"I want to go in," said Henry.

The Train Was Beginning To Climb

So, his father, feeling that he could trust Richard with the tall young man, went back to his seat.

When the next bend hid the mountains, Richard turned. Just as his hands left the brake, he stumbled and fell forward.

Before his head struck the door of the car, the tall man had caught him, and put him on his feet.

His sudden jump for Richard had thrown off the young man's straw hat, so it was dangling by the cord; and his glasses were so twisted that he looked very queer. But his eyes were smiling, as he looked down at Richard; and something in them seemed to say:

"Nothing bad really happened. I'm game, are you?"

Perhaps it was because Richard had been thinking about what his father had said about being brave all the time, perhaps it was something else; but whatever it was, though he was not over his fright, Richard's brown eyes telegraphed back to Mr. Bailey's blue eyes:

"I'm game, too!"

Mr. Bailey took Richard's hand, and they stood quietly together, looking down the track. After a moment, Richard looked up at Mr. Bailey, and they both smiled, as if they understood each other. Then they turned, and went back into the car.

"I should be glad to have you sit here with us," said Mr. Stanton, "but, if these boys begin to ask questions, they may prove lively company."

"Then," said Mr. Bailey, sitting down by Henry, "I'll ask a question first, for I couldn't help overhearing some of your talk with your sons. Are you interested in mines?"

"I'm very much interested in mines," answered Mr. Stanton," though I know very little about them. These boys are beginning to feel that they are real prospectors. We are on our way to the Comstock mines."

"I'm going to the Comstock myself," said Mr. Bailey, handing Mr. Stanton his card. "Do you know anybody there?"

"I have a letter to a man in charge of a mine," answered Mr. Stanton, giving Mr. Bailey his own business card. "I hear it isn't an easy thing to get a permit to visit the mines."

"No, Mr. Stanton, it isn't easy; but they have just sent for me to come to examine a new vein, so I think I can arrange for you to see one of the mines."

"How can you tell where there is gold?" asked Henry, who had slipped into the seat with Mr. Bailey.

"In the first place," said Mr. Bailey, "I just look at the rock. Quartz rock is what we look for here; that's the kind that generally has gold in it. It is a kind of rock that looks like smoky glass."

"We have some quartz crystals at home," said Mr. Stanton, "so the boys have some idea of quartz."

"Then after that," said Richard.

"Well, I pound it up fine, and look at it again. Sometimes I can see tiny pieces of gold; but there is generally so little gold in the rock that we can't find it till we test it with mercury."

"What is mercury?" asked Henry.

"Open your mouth a minute, and let me look in it," said Mr. Bailey. "Yes, you've had a tooth filled with gold, and there's one that has been filled with something dark. That one has mercury in it."

"The dentist didn't tell me that," said Henry.

"I suppose he said 'amalgam,'" said Mr. Bailey, "for he

mixed something else with the mercury. If you're going to be a prospector, you must understand what 'amalgam' means; and it's not very hard to understand, either, for it simply means that mercury unites easily with gold and silver. If we pound the rock up, and mix mercury with the pieces, the mercury will unite with the gold and silver, and separate them from the rock."

"What does mercury look like?" asked Richard. "Is it black?"

"It looks like silver, and is sometimes called quicksilver. It is what they put on the back of mirrors. I think you must have seen it in thermometers, too."

"I know," said Henry. "I broke a thermometer once, and that stuff ran out."

"It does run, something like water, when it gets a chance," said Mr. Bailey; "only it runs together, instead of going in all directions, as water does, when you spill it. After it picks the gold out of the rock, we heat the mixture very hot, and the mercury goes off in vapor, just as steam rises from water, and leaves the gold behind."

"They catch the mercury, and use it again, don't they?" asked Mr. Stanton.

"Yes, just as they condense steam."

"Where does mercury come from?" asked Richard.

"From mines, too. The miners say it takes one mine to run another. Almost all the mercury in the United States comes from California. It is so heavy that it is shipped in iron flasks. If we watch, we may see a car loaded with mercury on its way to the mines. There's something else that comes from California that they have to use to extract the gold from some kinds of ore. I wonder whether you could guess what it is."

"Coal," said Henry.

"Of course it takes a coal mine to help run a gold mine; but this is something that can be eaten. Perhaps it's hardly fair to ask you to guess. It is salt."

"Salt!" exclaimed Richard.

"That does seem queer, doesn't it? But when salt is roasted with some kinds of rock, something in the salt unites with the gold and extracts it from the rock. The chemists found that out a long time ago."

"Bed-time, boys!" said their father.

"Mayn't we have a story first?" asked Henry.

"Perhaps Mr. Bailey will tell you one, if that isn't asking too much."

"Let me see," said Mr. Bailey. "I think I'll tell you the first story I heard about gold, when I was a little boy."

"Please do," said Henry, sitting up close to Mr. Bailey, and putting his hand through Mr. Bailey's arm.

"Once upon a time, there was a king named Midas, who helped the god Bacchus to find the old man that had brought him up. Bacchus was so glad to find his foster-father, that he told Midas he would give him anything he wanted. So Midas thought and thought about what he would like most to have; and, at last, told Bacchus that he would like to have everything that he touched turn to gold.

"Bacchus was very sorry to have him ask a thing like that; but he told Midas that he might have his wish.

"When Midas reached home, he ordered a great feast of all the things that he liked best. But the first thing he tried to eat turned to gold, as soon as it touched his lips; and then he tried to drink something, but that, too, turned to gold.

There he was, with gold all around him, but nothing to eat or to drink, and in danger of starving to death.

"Then he went to Bacchus, as fast as he could, and asked him to take the gift back. Bacchus told him to bathe in the river Pactolus. As soon as Midas touched the bottom of the river, the sand turned to gold, and that was the end of his power to change things to gold."

"Father said that river was where Croesus got his gold," said Richard.

"But that isn't a really truly story," said Henry.

"It is, and it isn't," said Mr. Bailey. "We don't suppose, of course, that there was really any god Bacchus; but Midas was a king, and I suppose he had so much gold that people said that everything he touched, turned to gold."

"It means that gold alone couldn't make a man happy," said Mr. Stanton; "so it's a really truly story, after all. Now, boys, say good-night."

"Good-night," said Mr. Bailey, "and pleasant dreams about the things we are going to see."

Up and up, and over the mountains, through the forty miles of covered sheds that keep the winter snow of the Sierras off the railroad tracks; then down again, going in a few hours a distance that had taken almost as many days, when the California miners went across the Snowy Mountains, in the silver rush of '59, on and on the train carried them towards the famous Comstock mines.

CHAPTER IV

THE SILVER STATE

HE next morning, a tiny sunbeam that stole in by the edge of the curtain, touched Henry's eyes, and told him to wake up.

It took him a minute or two to find out where he was; then he thought that it would be great fun to wake Richard and his father. He wanted to wake Mr. Bailey, too, but he wasn't sure that he knew Mr. Bailey well enough to do a thing like that.

He touched Richard's arm, and called softly, "Dick, Dick!"

Richard opened his eyes, and started to speak, but Henry said, "Don't say anything loud enough for father to hear. I want to see if we can't get dressed first, and surprise him."

"That'll be great," said Richard, "if we can do it; but it will be hard work to get down without waking him, for he's right under us."

"Let's try it, anyway," said Henry.

They both sat up, and tried to find their clothes. The things didn't seem to be just where they had left them; but they found one thing after another, until Henry said:

"I've lost one shoe, but I have all my other clothes."

"Never mind," said Richard, "we can't put our shoes on till after we get down, anyway, so let it go."

On the way down, Richard dropped a shoe, and Henry dropped his coat; but, when they peeped through the curtains of his berth, they saw that their father was still fast asleep.

The porter saw them coming, and smiled so broadly that they both smiled back, as he opened the door of the dressing room, and said:

"Want any help, young gentlemen?"

"Thank you," said Henry; "we don't need any help now; but, after we have waked our father, I should like to have you find my other shoe. It's mixed up with the things in the berth."

"Let me know when you're ready, and I'll find it," said the porter. "You're not the first boy that has lost a shoe in his berth; and I'm sure you won't be the last. You ought to have put them down on the floor, and then I'd have shined them all up for you."

They both hurried as fast as they could; but, somehow, their clothes didn't seem to go on so easily as they did when their father was around to help them. Henry lost his collar button; and, when he asked Richard to help him, Richard said:

"Oh! you find it yourself. I can't stop to find it for you."

"I'm so afraid father will wake up, before we get back," said Henry.

"There it is, down under the radiator," said Richard, impatiently.

Having so many things go wrong had made Richard what mother called cross. Father called it by another name; he called it selfish. Richard didn't like father's name for the way he felt;

but, though he knew he might spoil Henry's good time, he kept right on dressing, and didn't offer to help Henry.

When Henry tried to brush his hair, the tears almost came into his eyes. Even father said it was hard to get the part straight, because there was a lock, way back, that always made trouble.

Richard had his hair brushed, and was ready to go out, when Henry said:

"Dick, won't you please help me? I can't get my part straight."

"It looks well enough," said Richard, opening the door. "We must hurry."

Then Henry, thinking of the fun they were going to have, forgot all about his hair; but Richard began to think more and more about it. He knew that his father would see right away, that he hadn't helped Henry; and he could just hear his father calling him selfish again.

"Dick," said Henry, "I don't know which is our berth; do you?"

Before Richard could answer, the porter appeared and said:

"This way. I'll show you where he is."

"You wake him, Henry," said Richard, now really ashamed of the way he had behaved; "it was your plan."

"Father, father!" said Henry, putting his hand gently on his father's face. "It's time to wake up. We are in Nevada now."

"Well, well," said Mr. Stanton, as soon as he was fairly awake. "What have you boys been doing?"

"We're dressed," answered Henry; "all but one of my shoes."

"So you are," said their father; "but, now that I look at you a little more carefully, it seems to me that Richard's necktie isn't on as straight as mother likes to see it; and the part in your hair doesn't go very far back; though, on the whole, you have done very well. Thank you for waking me. I want to see how Nevada looks."

Just then the curtains of the berth across the aisle were pushed back, and they saw Mr. Bailey.

"Won't you wake me up, too?" he asked. "I'm sure it must be very nice to have two boys to wake you up."

"It certainly is," said Mr. Stanton. "Good-morning, Mr. Bailey. I understand that we're in Nevada."

"We are," said Mr. Bailey, "and it's a fine place for prospectors. There's plenty of gold and silver here. If we hurry, we can get some seats in the dining car, where we shall have a good chance to see the country."

Not many minutes later, the boys were sitting by a broad window in the dining car, and Mr. Bailey and their father were ordering breakfast.

"It looks almost like the pictures of the desert in my geography," said Richard.

"That's right," said Mr. Bailey. "It used to be called the 'Great American Desert,' and nothing grew here but bunch grass and sage-brush and cacti with great thorns on them. You see even the mountains don't look the same, for they are steep and rocky instead of sloping down, as they do in California."

"Do you think there was once an inland sea here?" asked Mr. Stanton.

"Everything seems to look that way," Mr. Bailey answered. "They tell us that, a long time ago, the Atlantic and the Pacific were one ocean. Later, the mountains were thrown up, and that probably made this an inland sea."

"How long ago was that?" asked Richard.

"Thousands and thousands of years, for all we know," answered Mr. Bailey. "It took a long time for the earth to get into shape for men to live on it, you know."

"Such a desert must have been a hard place to cross, when the California rush was on," said Mr. Stanton.

"It certainly was; especially as there wasn't much water to be had, and what they found was full of alkali and often made the men and the animals sick."

"Didn't anybody live here then?" asked Henry.

"Nobody but horned toads and lizards and rabbits and crickets."

"I should hardly expect to find crickets in a desert," said Mr. Stanton.

"That has always seemed strange to me," said Mr. Bailey, "but there were hosts of them here."

"Settlers must have had a good deal of courage to come to a country like this," said Mr. Stanton.

"It took courage to come," said Mr. Bailey, "but it took more to stay. The men that came to Nevada in the silver rush had a harder time than they had in California — a good many of them came from California, you remember — because it was very cold the first winter that they were here."

"They were real heroes," said Mr. Stanton. "I think most of them must have been brave and unselfish."

Richard looked at his father to see whether he meant anything special when he said that; but his father was looking out of the window, and seemed just to be thinking.

"One thing is certain," said Mr. Bailey, "and that is, that being brave and unselfish is the first part of being a hero."

Richard looked at Mr. Bailey, and Mr. Bailey smiled, just as he had done the night before, out on the platform. Then he went on talking about the miners.

"There was a lot of snow that winter; and the tents and huts were so cold that the miners dug places in the sides of the hills to live in. Sometimes they moved into a place where they had mined out the ore; and, when they set up their stoves, they ran the stovepipes right up through the hill."

"When their chimneys smoked, the hill must have looked like a volcano," said Mr. Stanton.

"That's so," said Mr. Bailey, "and I have no doubt there was plenty of smoke. Some of the miners cooked in sage-brush huts. They had to do their own cooking, because there were no women to do it for them; and the boarding-houses charged so much that they couldn't afford to live in them. They cooked in coffee-pots and frying pans. Comstock, the man for whom the whole lode or vein was named, used to be called 'Pancake,' because he made so many pancakes. He said he was too busy to make bread."

"Are we almost at the mine?" asked Henry.

"One more stop," answered Mr. Bailey, "and we shall be there. I'm going through to the baggage car, now, to look up my outfit."

Two hours later, the party stood on the steps of the hotel, looking at the town that had sprung up around the mine.

"What a queer-looking place it is," said Mr. Stanton. "I never saw a town before that was all built on the side of a hill. One man's living room seems to be on a level with the next man's cellar."

"They put the houses wherever they could find a spot large

enough for them to stand on," said Mr. Bailey. "They wanted to be near the mine."

"Father, mayn't Henry and I go down to the end of this street?" asked Richard.

"I don't know about that," answered his father. "You're in a strange place. What do you think about it, Mr. Bailey? Would it be safe?"

"If they won't go off the street," answered Mr. Bailey, "they would be safe anywhere around here; but, if they were to wander off on some side street, we might have to hunt them up."

"I can trust them not to go off this street," said Mr. Stanton, "and I think they'll be hungry enough to come back in time for lunch."

As they walked along, Henry said:

"Do you suppose, Dick, that there are any miners down in the ground under us?"

"I don't suppose there are any right under us," answered Richard, "for the street might fall through; but I shouldn't wonder if there were some in that hill over there. They're crawling around somewhere in the ground. I hope we shall meet some miners soon. I haven't seen anybody yet that looks like a miner."

"Isn't this a queer place!" said Henry, stopping in front of a large, low building where the door stood open.

"It's a blacksmith's shop," said Richard, looking in, "but I don't see any horses."

"Wouldn't you like to come in?" asked a big man, who wore a leather apron, and had a hammer in his hand.

"Do you suppose, Dick, that father would mind?" asked Henry.

"Not if we stay on this street," said Richard. "He likes to have us see things."

"If you will sit here," said the blacksmith, brushing the dust off a bench near his anvil, "you can see what I am doing."

"Where are the horses that are to have shoes put on?" asked Henry.

"We don't have many horses around here. Donkeys do better work in the mines, because they're smaller and stronger than horses are; but, if I didn't have anything to do but to shoe horses and donkeys, I should have to go out of business."

"What do you do?" asked Richard.

"I mend and sharpen the pickaxes and drills for the miners," answered the blacksmith. "Smashing rocks is pretty hard on tools. Here's a new lot coming; and here is a donkey, too."

"He's bigger than any donkey I ever saw," said Henry.

"They take pretty good care of him, don't they?" said Richard.

"Have to take good care of animals, as well as of men, if you want them to do good work," said the blacksmith, hammering away on a red-hot pickaxe that he had just taken from the fire.

"I reckon they've struck a hard place in the rock to-day, from the looks of this pick. Just look at it," he went on, holding up a pick that had one side broken off short.

"Do the men have to wait for you to mend their picks?" asked Henry.

"Hardly, sonny," said the big man smiling. "They have men in the mines that go around, like express men, to get all the broken picks and drills, and to give the men good ones. See whether you can lift that," he said, holding out the pick.

Richard tried with both hands, and had hard work to lift it; then Henry tried, but it was too heavy for him.

"That's pretty heavy," he said.

"Now try a hammer."

Richard tried with one hand, but could not lift it.

"Take both hands," said the blacksmith. "That's the way the miners do."

"Then how can they hold the drill?"

"It isn't like holding nails. It takes two men. One man holds the drill, while the other strikes it; then they change places, and the other man takes the drill."

"I should be afraid of my fingers," said Henry.

"The men are very proud of the way they drill," said the blacksmith. "They often have drilling matches on the Fourth of July; and the men from the different mines try for the prize.

"They take big blocks of granite, and put them outdoors where everybody can see the fun. They work so fast that you can't see when they change places with each other. My brother won in the last match. He struck seventy-five blows a minute."

"I should think," said Richard," that you would be proud of him."

"So I am," said the blacksmith.

"Miners have good times, don't they?" said Henry.

"Fourth of July comes only once a year, sonny. There's a good many days of hard work in between Fourths. Sometimes there's other things, too—accidents, I mean. You boys ought not to hear about accidents; but I tell you my brother was brave, last time. He was a hero, a real hero," said the blacksmith, bringing his hammer down hard.

"What do you think makes a hero?" asked Richard.

"I don't know as I ever thought about *making* a hero," said the blacksmith, wiping his forehead with a big red and yellow handkerchief. "But, now that I do think of it, I should say that a hero would *have* to be brave."

"Anything more?" asked Richard.

"Well, I think," said the blacksmith, slowly, stopping to wipe his forehead again; "I think he'd have to think of the other fellow first."

"That's what my father says," said Richard; but he said it as if he had been hoping that the blacksmith would say something else.

"It looks that way to me," said the blacksmith, "now that I think of it. My brother did that; and he saved ten men."

"We must be going," said Richard. "Father may think that we are lost."

"Another donkey!" said Henry, when they reached the door.

"He's a good-looking one, too," said Richard.

"But we don't have any donkeys around here now, that are so smart as one that my father used to tell about," said the blacksmith.

"What did he do?" asked Henry.

"He was feeding on the hill over there beyond that tall tower that you see, just above the mill; and the wind blew so hard that it took him off his feet, and carried him right through the air to the hill on the other side, and he got up and went to eating again."

"I never heard of anything like that," said Richard. "I should like to hear you tell some more stories; but we must go now."

"Call again!" said the blacksmith.

"Thank you," said Richard; "we have had a very nice time."

"Well, boys," said Mr. Bailey, at lunch, "what did you see?"

"We saw a hardware store, and a dry-goods store, and a big lumber yard, and most every kind of a store," answered Richard.

"And we called on a blacksmith, and he told us a story about a donkey," said Henry.

"A blacksmith!" said Mr. Stanton.

"You see, father," said Richard, "they have to have blacksmiths to sharpen tools for the miners."

"The blacksmiths used to make more money than the miners did, when the mines were first opened," said Mr. Bailey. "By the way, Henry, what donkey story did the blacksmith tell you?"

"About one that blew over to another hill."

"I thought so. That is an old Comstock story. That is a really truly story, Henry, so they tell me."

"I was disappointed not to see a single miner," said Richard.

"Didn't you meet any men at all?" asked Mr. Bailey.

"There were a lot of men on the street; but nobody that looked like a miner. They looked more like you and father."

"I have no doubt that you saw a lot of miners. They dress very well when they are off duty. They don't wear miner's clothes except when they are in the mines. We will go to see them in their mining clothes, before very long; but not to-day, for we're all going to ride this afternoon."

"Where?" asked Henry, reaching up to take hold of Mr. Bailey's hand, as they went down the corridor.

"Ah, you'll *see*," said Mr. Bailey.

CHAPTER V

PROSPECTING ON THE HILLS

ANYTHING the matter, Richard?" asked Mr. Stanton, when, soon after lunch, he and Henry went up to their room, and found Richard sitting by the window.

"I'm just thinking, father," answered Richard.

Then his father knew that Richard had something on his mind, so he went on talking with Henry.

Richard was thinking of what the blacksmith had said about the second part of being a hero. It seemed queer, right in the midst of such a good time, to have to stop to think about a thing like that. But here was the blacksmith, and here was Mr. Bailey, too, talking so that they had made him think hard about the very thing that he and his father had had a long, special talk about just before they left home.

Richard had tried, almost ever since he could remember, to be brave; that was worthwhile. But trying to be unselfish was a very different matter. It was something that you had to keep on your mind all the time; and it was likely, any time, to spoil a lot of fun.

Richard sat still for six whole minutes. His father knew how long it was, for he looked at his watch. Then he got up, and said very pleasantly:

"Father, would you like to have me go down to get you a paper?"

"Thank you, Richard," answered his father; "I have one."

His father knew, right away, that Richard had made up his mind to try to be unselfish, for getting a paper was one of the things that he didn't like to do when he was at home. But, of course, he didn't tell Richard that he knew; he only said:

"I think Mr. Bailey may be waiting for us to come down. He said that he would meet us on the piazza."

When they reached the corner of the piazza nearest the street, they found the case that contained Mr. Bailey's outfit, but no Mr. Bailey.

"I should like to know what there is in that case," said Richard.

"I tell you what I wish," said Henry. "I wish he'd take us with him. I think it would be a lot more interesting than going down in a dark mine."

Just then a strange-looking man came around the corner of the hotel, and stopped at the sidewalk, as if he were expecting somebody to come for him.

He had a queer hat on his head, for it was made of shiny yellow stuff; and, at the back, it had a sort of cape that hung down below the collar of his brown flannel shirt. He carried a long roll of something on his shoulders; and he had a blue sweater rolled up, and fastened around his waist.

A Strange—Looking Man

Queerest of all, he had a coffee-pot hanging from one side of his belt, and a tin cup from the other. His brown trousers were tucked into tall russet boots that had heavy soles with a lot of nails in them.

"Is that a miner, father?" asked Richard.

"I guess he's an Indian," said Henry.

"We might go down the walk," said Mr. Stanton, "and see whether it's best to ask him who he is, and where he is going."

"Let's," said Henry; but he was careful, as they went down, to keep on the side farthest away from the man.

"Pardon me, sir," said Mr. Stanton, touching the man's arm, "my boys—"

Before he finished the sentence, the man turned around, and the boys saw another queer thing hanging from a strap on his belt. It was a sort of round tin box, and had a cap screwed on the upper edge where the straps were fastened.

As the man did not speak, the boys looked up, and saw neither a miner nor an Indian, but a smiling face with two blue eyes, twinkling behind a pair of glasses.

"Mr. Bailey!" shouted Richard.

"Mr. Bailey, prospector," said Mr. Stanton, taking off his hat, and making a bow.

"Aren't you going to speak to me, Henry?" asked Mr. Bailey, his eyes still twinkling.

"Yes, sir," said Henry; "but—"

"Do you think you'll have to get acquainted with me over again? I didn't realize that you were the kind of boy that would mind a man's clothes."

"No, sir; but—"

"I must admit," said Mr. Stanton, "that, if I hadn't known

who you were, I should almost have hesitated about speaking to you."

"I shouldn't have blamed you," said Mr. Bailey. "I hardly knew myself the first time that I wore these things; but I'm so used to them, now, that I feel more at home in them than in anything else."

"What's that thing?" asked Henry pointing to the round metal box.

"That's a canteen for water," answered Mr. Bailey. "I don't suppose you know what it is to be very, very thirsty. That's one of the things that prospectors have to look out for. I've been caught, once or twice, without water; and I don't know when I ever suffered more. Here's our wagon. I'm going to take you out to the hills with me."

"Goody!" exclaimed Henry; "that's just what I was wishing."

"If you wish for the right thing," said Mr. Bailey, "your wish often comes true. I'm sure this was one of the right things for me, as well as for you."

"Now, I'm going to take off some of these camping things. I can walk in them all right, but they're not very comfortable to ride in."

"Perhaps you'll help me, Henry, to fold up this cap. It's oilskin, you see, and I have to be careful of it. I don't need it out here, in the summer, anyway; but I'm glad enough to have it in rainy weather."

"There goes the blanket," he went on, tossing it into the wagon.

"Blanket!" exclaimed Richard. "I thought it was some kind of rubber tire."

"That's not bad!" said Mr. Bailey. "It's a blanket strapped

into a rubber cover to keep it from dust and wet. It's easier to carry, too."

Mr. Bailey put on his straw hat; the driver put the outfit case into the wagon; and off they drove. Henry sat in front with Mr. Bailey and the driver; and Richard sat behind with his father and Mr. Denton, the young man from the mine, who was going to show Mr. Bailey the new vein that they wanted him to examine.

The road went up hill, almost all the way; and it was so rough that they had to hold on to the wagon to keep from falling out. The ride was a long one, too; and they were glad when it was over, and they reached the foot of the hill near the new vein.

"We shall have to do some climbing, now," said Mr. Denton. "There is a flat place, higher up, where you can pitch your tent."

Mr. Stanton hung the long roll of blanket around his neck, and took a large covered basket from under the seat; Henry carried the coffee-pot and the cup; Richard took the sweater and the canteen; and Mr. Bailey took his outfit case.

Then Mr. Denton started ahead with a folded tent under his arm; and the driver, carrying the rest of the things, brought up the rear.

It was a steep climb; but, at last, they reached a broad flat place where Mr. Denton halted.

"This," he said, "seemed to me the best place to camp."

"It certainly is a good place," said Mr. Bailey, looking carefully around. "The first thing, now, is to find out where we are. I like to pitch my tent so it faces east."

"See Whether I Can Do It"

He took a small round box from his outfit case, touched a spring, and open it flew.

"That's a compass," said Richard. "I never saw a real one before; but there's a picture of one in my geography."

"That geography of yours seems to be a most remarkable book," said his father, smiling.

"I think," said Mr. Bailey, "it must be because Richard is specially interested in geography that he finds so many things in his book. If he weren't, he wouldn't learn much, even if he had the best geography in the world. Now then, this way is east; we'll put our tent right here."

"I don't suppose there are any bears around here," said Henry, looking up the steep hill.

"I don't think there are any," said Mr. Bailey. "I have never seen one, since I began to prospect; but, if I did meet one, I should be ready for him. I make it a point to practise with this," he went on, taking a revolver from his pocket.

"I should like to see you practise," said Henry.

"There isn't much here to shoot at," said Mr. Bailey. "Let me see. There's a stray cactus over there; perhaps I could take off the end of a leaf. Watch and see whether I can do it," he said, taking careful aim.

"There it goes," said Henry, as the end of the leaf fell to the ground.

The boys had been so busy watching Mr. Bailey, that they were surprised, when they turned, to see that a fire was blazing on a flat rock, and that their father was taking one package after another from the big basket.

"Are we going to stay here for supper, father?" asked Richard.

"Yes, my son; and, now, I'll tell you a little secret that Mr. Bailey and I have kept since yesterday morning. We're going to spend the night here, and sleep in Mr. Bailey's tent."

"Won't that be fun!" exclaimed Richard.

"More fun than we've ever had," said Henry, throwing up his cap.

After they had eaten their supper, they sat by the campfire, and watched the sun as it sank behind the pointed mountains. Then they watched the fire, until Mr Bailey said: "Turn around, to see what I have to show you!" Wondering what it could be, they turned, and saw, far across the desert, the round face of the full moon coming slowly up over the hills.

They watched it for some time without saying a word. Then Mr. Stanton turned to Mr. Bailey, and said:

"I think we have a great deal to thank you for, Mr. Bailey. I have seen the moon rise in many places; but I never saw it rise like this. I am sure the boys will always remember this wonderful sight."

After Mr. Denton and the driver had gone down to the wagon, the boys went into the tent, and their father rolled each of them up in a blanket, and put them close together on the ground, so as to leave a place for himself, for the tent was very small.

"What are we going to do to-morrow?" asked Henry, when Mr. Bailey looked in to say goodnight.

"Going to see what's in the new vein," answered Mr. Bailey. "That's what we came up here for, you know."

"There isn't any tent for you to sleep in," said Richard.

"My blanket is enough for me," said Mr. Bailey. "I often sleep in the open air. That's part of being a prospector."

The next morning the boys slept so late that their father had to waken them. After unwinding their blankets he set them on their feet.

"I'm stiff," said Richard.

"So am I," said Henry, "but we're having so much fun that I don't mind just being stiff."

Down below them, on the hillside, they saw Mr. Bailey with a canvas bag in his left hand, and a hammer in his right, springing from one rock to another, and stopping, now and then, to knock off pieces of the rock, which he put in his bag.

When he saw them, he waved his hammer, and started back. He was much farther away than he seemed to be; for, by the time that he reached them, the boys had finished their breakfast.

"I have some fine specimens for you, boys," he said as he came up. "I'm going to empty the bag on this canvas; and I want you to look the pieces over, and see what you think have gold in them."

When Mr. Bailey came back with his outfit case, Henry held up one of the larger pieces of rock.

"I think this one is gold," he said. "It's sort of yellow, and it's heavy. The driver said that gold is heavy."

"I took this one," said Richard, holding up his piece, "because I think it is quartz; and you told us that the quartz out here generally has gold in it. Besides, I think I can see some little yellow specks on one side."

"Aren't you going to choose a piece, father?" asked Henry.

"No. I'm going to sit here and watch the testing."

"We'll try yours first, Henry," said Mr. Bailey, taking from his case something that looked like a little cup. "We'll pound off some pieces and put them in here."

When the bits of rock were ready, he lighted a candle and took out a long metal tube, saying: "I want you to watch carefully, Henry, while I blow through this tube."

Henry stood close to Mr. Bailey, and watched him, as he blew the flame from the candle on the pieces in the cup.

"It doesn't smell very nice," he said.

"That's right," said Mr. Bailey; "it doesn't, because there's sulphur in it, and that's one of the things that I wanted you to notice."

Mr. Bailey kept on blowing, till there was only a little round ball left in the cup. Then he took a magnet out of the case, and said:

"See what this will do to it, Henry."

Henry looked very much surprised when he found that the magnet took up the little ball. Then he looked a little disappointed, and said: "That's just the way the magnet sticks to my new jackstraws, at home."

"Then what is your specimen?" asked Mr. Bailey.

"I suppose it's iron," said Henry, looking still more disappointed.

"That's what it is," said Mr. Bailey; "but you have learned one of the first things that every prospector has to learn; and that is, that 'all that glitters is not gold."

"There's probably a little gold in it, for that kind of iron often contains a small amount. You're not the first person that has mistaken it for gold. This kind of iron has deceived so many men, that the miners sometimes call it 'fool's gold.' The real name is iron pyrites.

"Now, I want you to look at your piece of rock again, and see how beautiful it really is. It's made up of tiny little cubes."

"Perhaps Mr. Bailey will let you have that specimen," said Mr. Stanton, patting Henry on the shoulder. "Then we will take it home, and add it to our collection of minerals."

"Surely!" said Mr. Bailey. "That's just the thing to do. It's a fine specimen. I'm glad you are making a collection, for that's the best way in the world to begin to study rocks."

"Now, Richard, pound up your specimen, and we'll begin on that."

This time Mr. Bailey took a small iron flask from his case, and poured some mercury on the bits of rock. Then he washed the mixture in a tiny pan; dried what was left in the bottom on some blotting paper; and put it into the cup.

"You do this testing so easily," said Mr. Stanton, "that it looks very simple; but I suppose it took you a long time to learn to test minerals."

"Yes," said Mr. Bailey. "I was just going to tell the boys that there's something that isn't in my case that has to be put with all these things, if one is going to be a prospector; and that is a lot of patience. I rather think these boys have some, for they've kept very still."

After he had worked a little longer, Mr. Bailey said:

"Watch, Richard, while I blow."

"It looks black," said Richard; but in a minute he shouted: "It's turned yellow, it's turned yellow!"

"When it does that, we say it 'winks,'" said Mr. Bailey. "Then we know that we have gold, and we call the bead a bullion bead. That means that it isn't pure gold. It's the kind of gold, though, that they send away from the mines."

"I think," said Mr. Stanton, taking out his watch, "that I had better begin to pack up our things. It's about the time that Mr. Denton said he wanted us to come down."

"I've decided to go back with you," said Mr. Bailey. "I want to report what I have found; and, besides, the superintendent said that, to-morrow morning, he would take us over one of the mines."

CHAPTER VI

DOWN IN THE MINE

WHENEVER we start out to go anywhere in this town," said Richard, "even to going down in a mine, we have to climb a hill."

"That's true," said Mr. Bailey; "the hills make work for us, and for the miners, too; but, in the long run, the mining engineers make the hills do a lot of work for the mines."

"I don't see how hills can work," said Richard, a little doubtfully.

"If you will look over on the sides of the mountains, you will see something that looks like covered railroad tracks. Some of those lines are pipes for bringing water to the mines, and some are flumes for bringing wood.

"It takes a lot of water to run a mine, and there was no good water here for the men to drink, so they brought the water down from the mountains.

"They need a great deal of lumber, too, in the mines, and it would be almost impossible to get it down from the mountains, if they had to depend on men and horses; so the engineers built those long wooden troughs we call flumes, and the water in the flumes brings the logs down to the mills. You see, the mountains really work for the mines.

"There are some other things that the hills, right here, do for the mines. If you keep a sharp watch, you will see what I mean."

Up the hill they went, until they reached a building with a tall tower.

"This," said Mr. Bailey, "is the place where we shall find the elevator. The mine is so deep that the elevators need large, strong frames."

"Passes, sir," said the man at the door, looking at the boys as if he did not intend to let them in.

"Here they are, four of them," said Mr. Bailey. "I know that you don't often admit young men like these; but I am sure they will be as much interested in the mine as we shall be."

"We are evidently just in time," said Mr. Stanton, when they reached the elevator, and saw the men standing in line.

High up, on a platform, sat a man with a lever in his hand; and on the front of the platform was a big sign, "Don't speak to the engineer."

"Every time that I come here," said Mr. Bailey, "I'm glad that I'm not in that man's place. Too much depends on that engineer for any man ever to want the place. A wrong move of the lever might mean death to the men below."

They watched the engineer, as he slowed the car down, and finally brought it to a stop; and they watched the men, coming off one by one.

The men wore only flannel shirts, shoes and trousers, and

each man carried a pail. They moved very quietly, and went into the rooms at the right of the large room.

Just as quietly, from the left, came more men ready to go down. They were dressed like the men that had come up, and they also had pails; but each of these men had a candle in his hand.

"Now," said Henry, "we've seen some real miners."

"Do they change their clothing here?" asked Mr. Stanton.

"Yes, they do," answered Mr. Bailey. "This is a mine where it is unusually warm, so the men change here."

"They seem strong," said Mr. Stanton, "but they look very different from men that work out of doors. Their complexions are almost pink and white."

"But they have strong nerves," said Mr. Bailey. "I don't believe that there are any braver men in the world than the men in the mines."

When the last man of the morning shift had gone down, the superintendent of the mine came to Mr. Bailey and said that he would take them down with him on his tour of inspection.

"Would the boys like to take candles?" he asked.

"I should like to," said Richard.

"You may carry the candle, and I'll take charge of the matches," said his father.

"Before we go down, I want you all to take a look at these cables," said Mr. Bailey, pointing to the top of the car.

"They're steel wire outside, and hemp rope inside," said the superintendent. "That makes them strong and makes them wind easily on the drum.

"The indicator shows that the cage is almost here," he went on, "and the electric signal will ring in a minute."

When they saw the elevator empty, they did not wonder that the superintendent had called it a cage, for it was open on two sides, and had only bars on the other two.

As they stepped on the car, Henry took hold of his father's hand and held it so close that his father said:

"All right, little son?"

"All right, father, as long as I have hold of your hand," answered Henry, trying to be very brave.

"At which station are we going to stop?" asked Mr. Bailey.

"Station number eighteen. Perhaps your friends do not know that our stations are a hundred feet apart, so that means eighteen hundred feet down."

"I don't see any rocks," said Richard. "I thought I should see rocks through the sides of the elevator, but it's all wood."

"If you could see rocks," said the superintendent, "we shouldn't be very safe, for they might fall into the elevator. We have to keep rocks and water out, so we always line the shafts with wood, as we sink them."

"Station eighteen!" called out Mr. Bailey, when the car stopped.

"I'm going to telephone to the engineer," said the superintendent, "so that he'll know that we are all right."

"Telephones and electric lights," said Mr. Stanton, glancing around the big room at the landing, "make the mine seem like a city underground."

"That's what a mine really is," said the superintendent. "Our main street runs north and south. We call it Broadway.

You can travel several miles in some of the mines. We have plenty of side streets, too."

"This room makes me think of a store," said Richard, going over to some kegs that stood at the back of the room.

"I hope I shan't frighten you," said the superintendent, "if I tell you that those kegs have dynamite and powder in them. You see, we have to blast the rock to help the miners along."

When Richard heard the word "dynamite," he gave a little jump and hurried back to his father as fast as he could.

"Dynamite always sounds dangerous," said Mr. Stanton. "I don't think I should care to stand by a keg of it, myself."

"But, as a matter of fact," said the superintendent, "it's much safer to handle, under ordinary conditions, than powder is, and it's safer to store. I'll show you some."

In a moment he came back with a small scoop, which he had filled from one of the kegs.

The boys put their hands behind them and drew back as he came up; but Mr. Bailey smiled at them and motioned to them to look at the dynamite.

"What does it make you think of?" he asked.

"I know," said Henry. "It's like the brown sugar that mother puts into candy."

"We put this in large cartridges," said the superintendent, "and we fire them by electricity, so there is little danger, unless the men are very careless. We try to put reliable men in these rooms, for we store the tools here, as you see."

"We saw the blacksmith," said Richard.

"Then you saw a very important man, for a great deal depends on him. The miners complain when their tools

Two Men Were Driving A Drill

are not sharp. If you will follow me down this track, I will show you where the miners are at work."

They had walked some distance in the dimly-lighted "drift," as the miners call the tunnel in the vein where they work, when suddenly they heard something that sounded as if the howling of the wind and the blowing of a trumpet had been mingled with some sort of an explosion.

Henry held his father's hand closer than ever; Richard took hold of Mr. Bailey's arm; and they all stood still.

In a moment they heard the sound again.

"What in the world is it?" asked Mr. Stanton.

"Don't be alarmed," said the superintendent. "That's only Tim, one of the donkeys. He has evidently heard us coming, for we are near the stable. Tim is a sociable sort of a fellow, so he has never liked to live down here. He always brays when he hears anybody coming."

"Do the donkeys live down here?" asked Henry, now quite brave again.

"We have to keep them down here. We take good care of them and give them plenty to eat and drink; but I wonder, sometimes, whether they like to live in the dark all the time. Here we are at the end of the drift."

They found themselves in a sort of cave with ragged walls, where two men were driving a drill, and two others were working with pickaxes. One of the men with a pickaxe wore a candle on the front of his hat, but the other men had fastened their candles to the walls of the cave.

"I didn't realize that candles would give so much light," said Mr. Stanton. "I expected to find lamps down here."

"We use lamps in some of our work," said the superintendent, "but they don't give a good light overhead. The candles throw light in all directions, and it's safe for us to use them, for we don't have the dangerous gases here that they have in the coal mines."

"These men with the drill are getting ready to blast. The men with the pickaxes are working where they blasted yesterday. Excuse me, while I go to examine this morning's blast.

"Here," said Mr. Bailey, after the superintendent had left them, "is the car that these men are filling. We shall have a chance to see Tim draw it back to the elevator landing."

"What is this pile of timber for?" asked Mr. Stanton, pointing to the end of the track.

"As fast as they take the rock out, they put timbers in to keep the walls from falling. It isn't safe to leave the space that they have mined empty."

"I have something to show you," called the superintendent. "Come over here."

They found him talking with three men who had pickaxes in their hands.

"She's a beauty, sir," said one of them, touching his cap to the party. "I've heard the old miners tell about finding such places, but I never saw one before."

"It's a sort of a jewel casket," said the superintendent. "It's not high enough for me to stand up in, so perhaps the young gentleman with the candle will go in, and show it to the rest of us."

"I didn't suppose that you would have a chance to use your candle, Richard," said his father, giving him a lighted match.

Holding his candle carefully in front of him, Richard stepped over the broken rock into the little cave.

"Oh!" he exclaimed. "Look, look!"

The others, standing as close to the opening as they could, echoed his exclamation, when they saw that the walls of the little room were covered with crystals of quartz. Blue, white, rose-pink, and purple, they flashed and glittered in the flickering light of the candle, until they almost dazzled their eyes.

Henry, quite forgetting that he was down in a mine, slipped through the opening and stood beside Richard.

"See!" he said, "there's a lot of gold in here!"

"We shall find some gold there," said the superintendent, "but most of what you see is iron and copper. We often find them with gold."

"All that glitters is not gold, you know," smiled Mr. Bailey.

"I know. Fool's gold!" said Henry.

"If you are ready to come out," said the superintendent, "I'll crawl in, and see whether I can find anything more."

In a minute he called, "If you will come in here, one at a time, I'll show you a rare sight, for here are some little nests of gold and silver wire."

"How do you account for things like that?" asked Mr. Stanton, when they were all safely out again.

"We don't pretend to account for them. We know, of course, something about how the crystals were formed; but nobody pretends to account for the wire. That's one of Nature's secrets.

"I'm glad to find this place in the mine. The old miners say that it always means that the vein will prove to be a bonanza."

"I wonder who first used that word," said Mr. Stanton.

"Some Spaniard, I suppose, long, long ago," said Mr. Bailey. "Its meaning is simple, for it is only the Spanish for success.

No matter how hard things go, the miners are always hoping that they will strike a bonanza."

A loud bray reminded them of Tim; and they went back to the track, where they found that the car was full, and that Tim was ready to draw it to the elevator.

"If you will follow Tim," said the superintendent, patting the animal on the head, "you will have a chance to see what we do with the loaded car."

Tim traveled slowly, as if he were afraid of losing good company; but they were not very far from the main shaft, and reached it just as the cage came down.

The man at the station unhitched Tim, let down the door of the landing-room, and pushed the car across it into the cage, then hooked the door up again.

Then he hitched Tim to an empty car and started him down the track.

"I feel sorry for Tim," said Henry, as they heard a final bray.

"So do I," said the superintendent, "and I shall be glad when we have more engines in the mine, and don't have to bring any animals down. We have trolleys in some parts of the mine. It's too hot, further down, for the animals, even though we use electric fans.

"We're mining twenty-six hundred feet down, and it would be too warm for the men if we didn't use electric fans and plenty of ice. Our bill for ice is one of our big bills."

"Is there much water down there?" asked Mr. Stanton.

"We keep the pumps working all the time, but we have the water under good control. We pump it up a thousand feet to the tunnel, and it runs off in that. We've had a good deal of trouble, in this mine, with hot water. Of course we expect to find water, but it is hard to control when it is hot."

"My geography says that it is hot, down in the earth," said Richard.

"We can stand by the geography in that," said the superintendent, smiling. "I'm wondering, now, whether I had better take you up, or go down further, and then come up to the tunnel."

"We haven't seen any of the large rooms," said Mr. Bailey.

"That's so. I'll take you down to station twenty-two. There's a very large one down there."

Down they went again and, getting off at station twenty-two, followed the superintendent until they came to a room, as the miners call the places where they have taken out all the ore.

"Here is a chance to see how they put those timbers together," said Mr. Bailey. "They call them square-sets, and they pile them up as you would pile blocks, only these are square frames, and that gives the men a chance to stand in them and work with safety."

"So much lumber must be dangerous, in case of a fire," said Mr. Stanton.

"It is so dangerous," said the superintendent, "that we sometimes seal the rooms, and shut them off from the rest of the mine. They burn like tinder when they once get started. We'll go down this drift, and take the elevator up to the tunnel."

CHAPTER VII

A TRIP IN THE TUNNEL

HE boys were really glad to take an elevator that was going up, instcad of down, for they were beginning to be tired of the dark; but, when the elevator stopped, they stepped out into a tunnel very much like the one that they had left. This one was larger than any that they had seen; and, between two rows of tracks, flowed a narrow river.

"This tunnel does several things for us," said the superintendent. "We not only sink shafts from here; but the water from the mines above flows down to the tunnel; and we pump it up here, from the mines below. That is what makes this river."

"I see that you have put in an electric line, since I was here before," said Mr. Bailey. "Do you have passenger service?"

"We don't have any passenger cars," answered the superintendent," but I think, if you are not afraid of your clothes, that I can give you a ride."

"We have more clothes at the hotel," said Mr. Stanton. "We want to see all that there is to be seen."

As they stood talking, a train of small cars, like the one that they had seen put on the elevator, came along. The superintendent signaled for the train to stop. After looking the cars over, he said:

"This happens to be a load of fine rock, and the cars are not so full as usual. That is fortunate for us, for it leaves more room in the cars. William," he called to the man at the station, "see if you can't find some empty bags."

When William appeared with some bags, the superintendent gave one to each of his guests. "If we take a car apiece," he said, "I think we can have a fairly comfortable ride. You may each select his own car. If you sit so that you can brace your feet against the side of the car, you'll be safe. I'm going to ride with the motorman."

"I've found a good place on the last car," said Richard. "There isn't so much rock in this one. I want to ride here."

"I don't know about that," said his father. "I think you had better come up further front."

"I can't fall off," said Richard, "for there's a lot of room here."

"He does seem to be safe," said Mr. Bailey, looking at Richard as he got into the car. "I think we can trust him to hold on. I'll sit in the car next to him."

"Very well," said Mr. Stanton. "I always feel sure that Richard will be careful."

When the train began to move slowly, the superintendent shouted:

"All right, back there?"

"All right!" answered Richard, taking hold of the sides of the car, and bracing his feet firmly in front.

After a minute or two, Mr. Bailey called:

"All right, Richard?"

"All right, sir!"

Just then the train struck a rough place in the road, and they were all well shaken up; but Richard was holding on so tight that he did not feel afraid of being thrown out of the car.

He had answered the call for the third time, when he noticed that Mr. Bailey's car seemed farther away than it had been. He found, too, that his own car was moving backward; and, before he knew what had happened, the train disappeared. His own car moved slower and slower, until it stood still.

The first thing that really happened, when Richard found that he was alone, was that a big lump came up in his throat, and filled it so full that he couldn't call for help.

But the next thing was, that he thought of his father, and that, somehow, made him feel safe; for he felt sure that his father would come back to get him.

When he thought of that, he wanted to behave so that his father would call him "brave little son." Richard had always remembered that that was what his father had called him the day when he broke his arm and didn't cry.

Besides, Richard had been hoping, for a long time, that he might have a chance to be a hero; and, of course, heroes don't cry.

Then he began to look around him. Up on the side of the tunnel, not very far away, was an electric light, shining brightly, as if it wanted to be company for him. He remem-

He Began To Wave

bered that once his father had told him just to wait, if he wasn't sure what to do. So he sat still, watching the tunnel river as it flowed on and on, and waited for his father to come.

Soon he heard a rumbling sound, and felt very sure that his father was coming; but, all of a sudden, he happened to think that it might be a train on the same track, and that it might run into him, so it wasn't safe to sit still.

Now the heroes that Richard had read about waved either flags or lanterns, when they wanted to stop a train. But he couldn't wave the electric light; and, in such a dark place, nobody could see anything so small as his handkerchief, even if he had a stick to put it on.

Rumble, rumble came the train from somewhere in the dark; and down got Richard, as fast as he could, and hurried back to the electric light.

When he reached it, he saw a little shelf of rock, just under it. He climbed up quickly, and began to wave his hat from side to side in front of the light. He remembered that his father had told him always to wave from side to side, because it wasn't easy to see things that were waved back and forth.

Nearer and nearer came the sound; and, just as Richard expected to hear a crash, the train stopped on the track on the other side of the narrow river.

"Hullo, there!" shouted the motorman. "Who are you, and how did you get here, anyway?"

"I'm Richard Stanton," said Richard, gaining courage as he saw the man smile, "and my car got unhitched from the superintendent's train. There it is down there."

"Don't often have young men traveling in private cars,

on this route," said the motorman, trying to keep his voice as cheerful as he could.

"They ought to have given you a special engine to run your private car. As they didn't, I reckon you'd better go back with me. The question, now, is whether you can jump across that river."

"That isn't much of a jump," said Richard; but he stopped to look at the river again.

"We don't take any chances, on this line, with young gentlemen that travel in private cars," said the motorman. "You just wait till I throw this rope across."

Richard caught the rope so easily that the man said: "I reckon that you belong to a baseball team. Now, the question is, can you tie a good knot, because I want you to tie that rope around you."

"My father showed me how to tie a good, hard knot," said Richard, as he tied the rope around his waist.

"All ready, jump!" shouted the motorman. And very glad was Richard, though he cleared the narrow river safely, to feel the arms of the big man around him, as he caught him and held him close for a minute, for he had a boy of his own.

"We can't make your car jump the river, so I shall have to take you in here with me. Perhaps you'll like it just as well as your private car," he said as he helped Richard up. "We'll pick up your car on the next trip."

"Didn't you meet the superintendent's train?" asked Richard.

"I passed them not very long before I found you. They'll be surprised when they find that your car got uncoupled. I'll warrant that your father will keep that telephone humming till we get to the station."

"I'm sure he'll try to find me," said Richard, in a tone that showed how sure he felt of his father's care.

"The super will tell him that I would be sure to pick you up and take care of you," said the man, showing in his tone how sure he was that the superintendent would trust him to do the right thing.

As they neared the station, they saw William waiting for the train.

"Seen anything of a stray car?" he called.

"Have the boy right here," shouted the motorman, while Richard waved his hat.

"Your father has rung us up once a minute for the last fifteen minutes," said William, helping Richard down. "He's pretty well excited, I tell you. I'll give you a box to stand on, so you can answer the telephone yourself the next time it rings."

Hardly had William fixed the box for him to stand on, before the telephone rang again, furiously, and Richard heard his father say:

"Have you found my son yet?"

"I'm right here, father," said Richard, "and I'm all right."

"Well, I am glad," said his father; but either the telephone wasn't in good order, or there was something the matter with his father's voice, for it didn't sound so clear as usual.

"We don't run another train out for an hour," said the motorman, taking out a big silver watch, "but the section boss is due here in a few minutes, and I think he'll let me run you out on a special."

When the section boss came along on his car, he looked

very much surprised to see Richard; but, before he had time to say anything, the motorman beckoned to him to come over to the other side of the room.

William talked with Richard until the section boss came back. He didn't say anything to Richard, but went right to the telephone and rang up the superintendent.

Then he came back to Richard, and said:

"I'm going to let this engineer"—Richard noticed that he said engineer—"take you out on my car. It won't take you very long to get back to your father."

Richard looked as if he would like to say a lot of things to the section boss, for he was very glad, but all that he did say was, "Thank you, sir."

So Richard and the big man got into the car, and Richard waved his hat as long as he could see William and the section boss.

They slowed down when they came to Richard's car, and the engineer fastened it so they could push it ahead of them. Then they ran faster, and soon Richard saw his father, who was starting down the track to meet him.

When Richard got off the car, his father held him, for more than a minute, closer than the engineer had held him. Then Henry and Mr. Bailey came up to welcome him too.

"Good-by, engineer," said Richard, putting out his hand. "I'm very much obliged to you for bringing me out."

"You're very welcome. Don't mention it!" said the big man, giving Richard's hand such a hard shake that he felt it for a long time afterward.

The engineer himself never forgot the hearty grasp that Richard's father gave his hand, just as he was ready to start.

But, when Mr. Stanton tried to put a piece of gold in his hand, he turned quickly away.

"You have done so much for me," said Mr. Stanton, trying once more to put the coin in the engineer's hand, "that I should like to do, even this little thing, for you. Perhaps you have a boy of your own. Won't you let me make him a little present?"

"That I have, sir!" answered the engineer. "Thank you, sir! I'll use the money for him. Thank you, sir!"

When the engineer had started back, Mr. Stanton, holding Richard's hand very tightly, as if he were afraid of losing him again, turned to Mr. Bailey and said:

"Now, we'll get somebody to take us back to the hotel as fast as we can go. We'll have something to eat, as soon as we get there; and then we will hear Richard's story."

They were at the table a long time, that day; and, after Richard had had so many good things to eat that he didn't want anything more, they all went up to Mr. Stanton's room.

While he was telling his story, Richard sat beside his father on a sofa. When he had finished, his father did just what Richard had hoped that he would do. He put his arm close around Richard, and called him, "brave little son."

"Weren't you scared a *bit*?" asked Henry.

"Not *very* much," answered Richard, for he felt that he must be sure to tell the truth. "I knew that father would try to find me."

"Prospectors ought always to be brave," said Mr. Bailey, "and, now that you've been tested, we know that you will be brave."

CHAPTER VIII

THE ORE MILL

I’VE been thinking, Richard,” said Mr. Bailey, at breakfast,” about the engineer that brought you out of the tunnel, yesterday. A man like that is worth knowing. All that he seemed to think about was to help you out of your trouble. I liked the way that he refused the money.”

“Till father spoke about his little boy,” said Henry.

“Then he thought of his little boy first,” said Mr. Bailey, “and that made it right for him to take the money. He is what I call an unselfish man.”

“This trip is showing me,” said Mr. Stanton, “that there are unselfish men everywhere. It is doing me good to see them for myself.”

“There have to be such men everywhere,” said Mr. Bailey, earnestly. “If there weren’t a lot of unselfish men in the world, it wouldn’t be a safe place to live in.”

Richard listened, but he didn’t say anything. He didn’t feel uncomfortable, either. Instead of that, he had a sort of warm feeling around his heart. Now that he had made up his mind to try, he was hoping that, some day, his father would say that he was unselfish.

"To-day, young prospectors," said Mr. Bailey, "I'm going to take you over the ore mill. That is where you'll have to use your chemistry."

"We don't know anything about chemistry," said Richard.

"I thought I gave you a lesson on the train."

"Oh!" said Henry, "that was about the mercury in my tooth."

"That was chemistry, only I didn't tell you very much about it. The chemists had to work a long time to learn all that they had to know in order to make an amalgam to put in your tooth. I'm going to give you another lesson, now; for, if I don't, you won't understand anything about what goes on in the mill."

"We'll listen," said Richard, "and try to understand."

"In the first place," said Mr. Bailey, "the atoms that the chemists talk about, are the smallest particles of matter that they can think of, too small for them to see.

"These atoms behave very much as people do: they like some atoms better than they like others. And, sometimes, when certain groups of atoms are such close friends that it seems as if they could never be separated, along come other atoms, and off go some of the first group, leaving their old friends all alone.

"Chemists spend a great deal of time just in trying to find out what atoms like each other. We couldn't get gold out of the rocks, if the chemists hadn't found out what other atoms the gold atoms like."

"You told us that they use mercury in the mines," said Richard, "so gold must like mercury atoms."

"Yes," said Mr. Bailey, "mercury atoms are specially good friends with gold, and with silver, too. Nothing but fire will really drive them off.

"There are some other things that, when they are mixed with water, dissolve the gold, and it disappears, as this sugar will when I put it in my coffee. The chemists say, then, that the gold is in solution; but they know what atoms to send after the gold to bring it back into grains again. That's all I'm going to tell you now."

"There's one question that I want to ask," said Mr. Stanton. "Is it as easy to get silver out of the rocks, as it is to get gold?"

"Silver is much harder to manage," answered Mr. Bailey. "The miners who first came here knew nothing about silver. They used to complain, when they were washing the gold out from the gravel and rock, that some 'blue stuff' carried off the mercury, and hindered their work. They threw the 'blue stuff' away, until a miner, who knew about silver, came and told them that they had been throwing silver away. That was really what started the silver rush."

Half an hour later, as they set out to walk to the mill, Mr. Stanton said:

"I suppose that we shall have to climb another hill. The hills may help the miners, but they make a good deal of work for us."

"It will be down hill, anyway, when we come back," said Mr. Bailey, laughing.

Up and up they went, and at last came to the mill, which stood just below the building where they had seen the elevator.

Some men were coming out of the door, and the boys started up the steps; but Mr. Bailey shook his head and kept on up the hill, until he reached the top of the building. There they saw the men tipping cars of ore over on one side, so that the rock could be dumped into large bins or boxes.

Then they went down to the floor below, and saw that the rock came through chutes to a great machine that made strange noises, groaning and crashing, as it crushed the rocks.

Down on the next floor, they saw that the fine crushed rock was being fed into big cans; and that in every can was a big weight, called a stamp, rising and falling so fast that they could not count the strokes.

"These cans," said Mr. Bailey, "have mercury in them, and every stamp weighs a thousand pounds. You will realize that the rock and mercury are well mixed together, when I tell you that the stamps fall a hundred times a minute."

"We seem to be doing some of our going down hill, right here in this building," said Mr. Stanton.

"So we are," said Mr. Bailey, looking hard at Richard, as if he expected him to say something.

"I see!" exclaimed Richard. "The things just fall from one floor down to the next. I've been watching, ever since you told us, to find out how hills can work. Now, I know!"

"Right!" said Mr. Bailey. "You've made a discovery, all by yourself. That's what I like to see boys do."

"I suppose we could use the term, force of gravity, instead of fall," said Mr. Stanton.

"I've heard about that!" said Henry. "That's what makes water run down hill."

"At any rate," said Mr. Bailey, "that's why they build ore

mills on the side of a hill. It saves a lot of hard work. They put the rock in, on the top floor; and they take the gold out on the lowest floor."

"How do they take the gold out?" asked Richard.

"They put the mercury with the gold in it, into big retorts, something like big kettles; then they put the kettles over the fire, and the heat drives off the mercury. The gold that is left behind looks like a sponge, for there are holes all through it. After all the mercury has been driven off, they generally melt the gold sponge, and pour it into molds that form it into bars."

"So far as I can see," said Mr. Stanton, "water is as necessary, here, as it was to the old placer miners."

"That will seem even more true," said Mr. Bailey, "when I take you over to the other mill where they use a process that is newer than the mercury process."

When they reached the mill, they met Mr. Denton at the door.

"I'm glad that I happened to be here," said Mr. Denton. "Wouldn't you like to have me take you over the mill?"

"Indeed we would," said Mr. Bailey. "I have never had a chance to go over this mill."

"This tank," said Mr. Denton, taking them over to a big tank at one side of the room, "holds the rock, that has been ground up with the cyanide solution instead of with mercury. That dissolves the gold; then we run it through a fine screen; and, after that, we filter it through sand, so as to take out the finer rock.

"After that we let it settle, until the top is clear; then we pour it off into another tank, and put in a lot of zinc shavings. The cyanide likes the zinc better than it does the gold, so it unites with the zinc, and leaves the gold, in little grains, behind."

"Boys, how is your chemistry holding out?" asked Mr. Bailey.

"Mine's all right," answered Richard. "It's just what you told us about this morning."

"Mine's all right, too," said Henry. "I can just see those atoms going off with the zinc, and leaving the gold behind."

"Well, well," said his father laughing, "that's rather more than the chemists are able to do. It's a good plan, though, to imagine that you can see a thing like that."

"Perhaps you will be a chemist, some day," said Mr. Denton. "There are plenty of things to be found out yet."

"I expect," said Mr. Bailey, "to learn something new every time that I visit one of these mills. That reminds me, Mr. Denton, that I didn't put down something that you told me the other day," he went on, taking out his note-book.

"Boys, what do you suppose that stands for?" he asked, pointing to a page with a circle, drawn in ink, at the top.

"I'm sure I don't know," answered Henry.

"That's the sign that the old Egyptians used for gold. They used the circle as the symbol of perfection, so they chose it for the sign of gold, because gold is the perfect metal."

"What does that new moon on the other page mean?" asked Richard.

"That's the Egyptian sign of silver," answered Mr. Bailey. "I like to use the signs."

"Egypt seems a long time ago," said Richard.

"The old Egyptian alchemists, as they were called, did live long, long ago. They were very much interested in gold, and spent years and years in trying to find something that they called 'the philosopher's stone,' that would turn other metals into gold."

"I think," said Mr. Denton, "that if those old alchemists could have done what our chemists can do to-day, when they get gold from the rocks, they would have felt that they had almost discovered 'the philosopher's stone.'"

"That is true," said Mr. Bailey. "They knew very little compared with what we know, but they managed to play some very clever tricks."

"What sort of tricks?" urged Henry.

"Well, the one that I happen to remember, just now," said Mr. Bailey, "is one that the Arabian alchemists used to do, way back in the time of the Arabian Nights stories. They put gold coins into mercury, and that made them look like silver. Then they showed the coins to people that came to see what they could do, and said that they could change them into gold.

"They put the coins into nitric acid, and boiled them. The hot acid dissolved the mercury, and left the gold as bright as ever."

"Then the Arabians knew some of the very processes that you use to-day," said Mr. Stanton.

"Yes; we owe them a great deal, for they discovered the acids for us."

"Are you going out to your camp this afternoon, Mr. Bailey?" asked Mr. Denton.

"I am going at two o'clock," answered Mr. Bailey, "and that means that we must hurry back to the hotel."

When two o'clock came, the boys and their father went down to the wagon with Mr. Bailey.

"You have done so much for us here," said Mr. Stanton, "that I hope you will come to New York, and let us do something for you. We shall look for a visit from you."

"Thank you," said Mr. Bailey. "I never know where I may be ordered next. If this vein proves to be a good one, I may have to go to New York to make my report in person."

"Do," said Henry. "Then you can come to stay with us."

"That would be very nice, I am sure," said Mr. Bailey, smiling." I think I shall begin to hope that I may come, for then I shall have something pleasant to think about, when I am all alone in camp."

Then they shook hands all around twice; and Mr. Bailey got into the wagon. They watched him, and waved their hats, until he disappeared around the corner.

"I'm sorry to see him go," said Mr. Stanton.

"He's the nicest man I ever saw," said Henry.

"Except father," said Richard.

"Thank you, Richard," said his father; "that's very loyal of you; but I like to have my sons know such men as Mr. Bailey. I certainly hope that he will come to see us."

"What are we going to do this afternoon?" asked Henry.

"We're going to sit right here on this piazza, just we three," said Mr. Stanton, leading the boys to a shady corner, and sitting down with one on each side of him.

"We all had a hard day, yesterday," he went on, drawing Richard closer to him. "Now, we can rest, and have a good talk about all the things we have seen. To-morrow we will go to Carson City with the superintendent, when he takes the gold to the assay office."

CHAPTER IX

GOLD BULLION

I KNOW one thing," said Henry, as they left the hotel, "I'm glad I'm going to the train, instead of going down in the mine."

"So am I," said his father, "but, if somebody hadn't gone down in a mine, we should probably not be going to the train."

"Why, father?" asked Richard.

"See whether you can't think why," answered his father.

"You don't mean money, do you?" asked Richard, after thinking a moment. "I shouldn't think it would be money, because you use most all paper money when you are at home."

"What's behind the paper, Richard?"

"The United States, of course," said Richard.

"You told us that once, don't you remember, father?" said Henry.

"So I did," said his father. "Well, then, I'm going to let you think about that why; and I'm going to add another to it. Why wouldn't there be any train to go to, if somebody hadn't gone down in a mine?"

"Coal, o' course, and iron, o' course," said Henry, quickly.

"What's behind the coal and iron?"

"I don't know," answered Henry.

"I know you don't," said his father, laughing. "Here we are at the station. I want you boys to stay outside and watch for the superintendent, while I buy the tickets."

"He's come," said Richard, meeting his father at the door. "He's down this way."

They found the superintendent, with four of his men, standing by the covered wagon that held the gold.

"Good morning," said Mr. Stanton. "I'm so much interested in this gold that I am really glad to see it again."

"It's in bags!" shouted Henry, who was peeping through the grating of the doors.

"Yes," said the superintendent, "most of the gold is handled in bags, or sacks, as we sometimes call them."

"Are you going to have your gold made into money?" asked Richard.

"No; I'm going to sell it to the United States; that is, I'm going to take it to the assay office, where they buy gold bullion. This gold isn't pure gold."

"Is the United States going to make it into money?"

"I presume that some of this gold will be made into money; and some of it will be made into—watches, for instance," answered the superintendent, who happened, just then, to take out his watch. "You seem to be very much interested in gold."

"The boys are trying to find out why we shouldn't have had our trip, if somebody hadn't been willing to work in a mine," said Mr. Stanton.

"Oh! I see!" said the superintendent, smiling down at

Richard. "When we get to Carson City, I'll take you to the assay office, so you can see what becomes of this gold. I'm afraid that, if all the gold were made into watches, even the United States wouldn't have money enough to buy them."

"I should think the United States could make enough paper money to buy almost anything," said Richard.

"I rather think," said the superintendent, "that you will have to take these boys to Washington, before they find the answer."

"All aboard!" shouted a brakeman.

The sharp tone of the man's voice startled Mr. Stanton so that he turned quickly, and stepped on the train. Henry, close behind him, hurried so fast that he struck the end of a seat with his suitcase; the fastening gave way, and out tumbled one thing after another.

The train had been several minutes on its way, before Mr. Stanton succeeded in collecting Henry's things. Then he realized that Richard was not with them.

"Did Richard get on the train with the superintendent?" he asked.

"I don't know," answered Henry. "I didn't look around."

"No," answered the superintendent, when Mr. Stanton found him, "he didn't get on with me. I saw him near the lower end of the platform, just as the train came in. He must have gone into the last car."

Then they went together to the very end of the last car; but they did not find Richard.

"What can have happened to him?" asked Mr. Stanton, excitedly.

"He probably got left," answered the superintendent. "We

can wire back, when we reach the next station. He's a bright lad. He'll take care of himself."

"I am to blame," said Mr. Stanton. "I ought to have seen that he got on ahead of me."

"I wouldn't worry, father," said Henry, when his father told him that they couldn't find Richard. "You know Dick is pretty good about getting out of scrapes."

In spite of his anxiety, Mr. Stanton smiled. Then he said:

"I must admit that he has a pretty good record along that line; but I wish he was safely out of this one. I don't know what your mother will say, when she sees only one boy with me."

"Mother!" exclaimed Henry.

"Yes; she and Edith are on their way to Carson City. She wanted to surprise you boys. Now, she's the one that will be surprised."

"I've seen the conductor," said the superintendent, coming back to sit with them. "He says he'll see that we have time enough to wire back; and he'll wire to the conductor of the next train to look after your son."

"We seem to be slowing down," said Mr. Stanton. "Is this the station?"

"This is only a flag station," answered the superintendent. "We don't often stop here."

Presently a brakeman came into the car, looked around a moment, and called.

"Mr. Richard E. Stanton!"

"Here!" said Mr. Stanton, starting down the car.

"Telegram, sir," said the brakeman, handing him a brown envelope.

Mr. Stanton tore it open and read:

"All right. Got left. Coming on next train."

Then Mr. Stanton laughed, partly because he was glad, and partly because he saw that the telegram was signed:

"Richard Eversley Stanton, Jr."

"He's paid for it, too," said Mr. Stanton. "I'm glad I gave him some money this morning."

It seemed to Henry as if the train never would reach Carson City. But it did, at last, and there were mother and Edith waving their handkerchiefs.

They were all so glad to see each other, that for a moment, Mrs. Stanton didn't miss Richard, then she began to look sober; but her husband told her Richard was coming on the next train. Then he showed her Richard's telegram, and she smiled.

"I'm thankful he's safe," said his father, "but I've made up mind that I shall have to be pretty severe with him. He ought to be more careful, and to think more about other people."

"Perhaps it was something that he couldn't help," said his mother.

"What in the world is this?" asked Mr. Stanton, feeling something hard in his hand, as he took his wife's wraps.

"Henry's umbrella," she answered, laughing. "I thought I had put it in the bottom of my big trunk; but, after we were all packed, Edith found it in the closet."

"Dear me!" said Mr. Stanton. "Now, we shall have to keep track of that. I did hope I shouldn't see it again, till we got back to New York."

"He may need it in Washington," said Mrs. Stanton.

"Washington!" exclaimed Henry.

"I've told a secret, haven't I?" said Mrs. Stanton, as she saw her husband shake his head. "I'm sorry!"

"Never mind," said Mr. Stanton. "They'll have something pleasant to think about. Now for a hotel," he said, calling a cabman.

When they reached the hotel, Edith, who did not want to leave her father, went into the office with him. They were waiting at the desk, when Mr. Stanton felt someone touch his arm. Turning, he saw the cabman that had brought them to the hotel.

"Umbrella, sir," he said. "I found it in the carriage.

"As Mr. Stanton put his hand into his pocket to give the man a coin, Edith took the umbrella.

"I'll take care of it, father," she said, "and give it to Henry."

"Thank you, Edith," said her father; "that will help me more than anything else you can do for me."

They had just finished lunch, and Mr. Stanton was taking his time table out of his pocket, when in walked Richard with a newspaper in his hand.

"Here's your paper, father!" he said. "I'm sorry I got left."

"Paper!" exclaimed Mr. Stanton.

"You see, father, I knew you would want a paper—you always do, you know. I saw a boy with some; and, before I got one, the train started."

Mr. Stanton looked at his wife; but he didn't say anything.

"I was afraid you'd be worried, father, so I sent the telegram right off."

Then Mrs. Stanton looked at her husband. That Richard should have sent the telegram, didn't surprise her, for, at home, telegrams were an every day matter; but that Richard should have thought of his father first, did surprise her. This Richard seemed a very different boy from the Richard that they had taken to California.

Mr. Stanton said:

"I think, Richard—"

But, before he got any further, Mrs. Stanton shook her head, slowly, and finished her husband's sentence.

"I think Richard must be very hungry," she said.

"Yes," said his father, calling a waiter, "and he'll have to hurry with his lunch, for it's nearly time for us to go to the assay office."

When they were ready to go out, Henry led the way.

"I know where it is," he said, "for there's a flag on it."

"Do they make money here?" asked Richard.

"They used to make it," answered his father. "They coined the first standard dollar here; but, now, they only buy bullion. The places where money is made, are called mints."

"You are using a great many words that are new to me," said Mrs. Stanton. "I don't know what bullion means; and I don't know what you mean by an assay office."

"Bullion here only means the gold as it comes from the mines, my dear," said Mr. Stanton. "There is always some silver with gold; they seem to like each other. There are generally some other metals, too, in the gold as it comes from the mines. 'Assaying is simply the process of getting the pure gold and silver from the bullion."

When they went into the building, they found the superintendent watching two men, who were weighing his bags of bullion.

"Can't one man be trusted to weigh gold?" asked Mr.

Stanton, when he saw that the second man was weighing the same bags that the first had weighed.

"They never allow one man to take charge of gold," answered the superintendent, "and we always see our own bullion weighed. The United States Government can't afford to have any mistakes made in its work."

"Are they going to give you gold money for your gold?" asked Richard.

"They won't give me anything, to-day, but a piece of paper that tells how many pounds of bullion I had," answered the superintendent. "When they find out how much pure gold and silver there is in the bullion, they will give me a check."

When the men had weighed the gold, they locked it up in a strong box, and took it to the melting room.

"We can see everything that they do, can't we?" said Mrs. Stanton, as they went down the long room.

"The government generally arranges things so as to give anyone that wants to a chance to see its work. All that the United States runs these assay offices for, anyway, is to help the mines."

"I was wondering why you didn't refine the gold at the mines," said Mrs. Stanton.

"It is much easier for us to bring it here; and it saves us a good deal of care, for we should have to watch it all the time. Besides, gold is the most valuable thing that the country can produce, so the government wants to handle it."

"It doesn't belong to the United States, does it?" asked Richard, who had listened to every word.

"Not until the United States buys it," answered the superintendent, smiling.

"I'm afraid, my son," said Mr. Stanton, putting his hand on Richard's shoulder, "that you are working too hard on that *why*. I don't want you to lose the pleasure of seeing these things. I'm going to give you something, in a few minutes, that will help you to find the answer. I want you now to look in here."

Over the railing they saw a small furnace, covered with a sort of a hood that had a little isinglass window in it. In a moment the workmen uncovered a large kettle, lifted it by a crane, and poured the hot melted gold into iron molds.

"After it is cool," said the superintendent, "they test the bars. They take little pieces of the bars, and two men make two tests, one from the top and one from the bottom of the bar. After they make their report, three other men reckon the value of the gold, according to prices on Wall Street."

"That's in New York," said Henry.

"And that's where father's office is," said Edith.

"The world is really very small, isn't it, when it comes to doing business," said Mrs. Stanton, shaking her head a little at the children to remind them that they mustn't talk about themselves."

"Now, children," said Mr. Stanton, when they reached the door, "I'm going to help Richard about this money question. I'm going to give each of you some paper money to keep till we get to Washington. Then you can find out for yourselves whether there is anything behind paper money."

"That's just the thing to do," said the superintendent, nodding at Mr. Stanton. "Just the thing to do."

"Here's a two-dollar bill for Richard; and here are two one-dollar bills for Edith and Henry."

"There isn't any bill at all left in my purse," said Mrs. Stanton, holding her little silver bag up by the chain, "so I shan't be able to find out anything."

"I know a very easy way for you to get some money," answered her husband, with a smile.

"Do you think that would help matters?" he asked, handing her a twenty-dollar bill.

"Very much," she answered, taking the bill.

"I shall put my bill in the inside pocket of my coat," said Richard.

"So shall I," said Henry.

"I'm going to let father keep mine," said Edith.

"Now, I'm going to get some of the kind of money that I want," said Mr. Stanton. "We're in the silver state, and I want some silver money. I'm going to let the rest of you go back to the hotel, while I go to the bank with the superintendent to get some silver money."

When Mr. Stanton reached the hotel, he had a small canvas bag of money in each hand.

"Are you going to carry all that silver back to New York?" asked Mrs. Stanton. "I should think you would rather have a bill."

"There's a special reason why I want this. I'll tell you some day."

That night, when they were all settled again on the train, Mr. Stanton told his wife about Mr. Bailey, and about Richard's being left in the tunnel.

"How you must have worried!" she said. Then, after thinking a moment, she added: "I'm glad Richard was brave."

"I feel very sure," said Mr. Stanton, after telling her about the day that Richard had sat still so long, "that, now, Richard is trying to be unselfish."

"That," said Mrs. Stanton, as if it was something that she had thought about a great deal," that would be worth the whole trip to California."

Two days later, after the boys had told their mother and Edith everything that they could remember about their trip, Richard said:

"Father, won't you tell us about the bags of silver?"

"I was just thinking about my silver money," answered his father, opening his traveling bag.

"I want you all to hold your hands, just as you do when we play, 'Who's got the button?' I'm going to give you some silver, and let you see what you can find."

"I have a half-dollar and two quarters, and some ten-cent pieces," said Mrs. Stanton. "I don't see but we all have the same kind of money."

"They're not all alike, in one way," said her husband. "I wonder whether any of you can find out what I mean."

"Is it a puzzle, father?" asked Edith.

"No. It's only something that calls for sharp eyes."

"I've found it!" exclaimed Henry. "There's a little bit of an S on one of my quarters."

"Mine isn't an S, it's an O," said Richard.

"One of mine has a D on it," said Mrs. Stanton.

"My ten-cent piece has an O, right under the bow knot," said Edith. "And my quarter has C, right under the eagle's tail."

"Anything more?" asked Mr. Stanton.

"Some of them are just plain, without any letter," said Richard.

"Then you have found all the different kinds," said Mr. Stanton; "so I'm going to tell you that the letters tell where the money was made.

"Every mint marks its gold and silver money. D stands for Denver; S stands for San Francisco; O for New Orleans; and C stands for Carson City, where they used to make money, as I told you."

"Some of mine are like Richard's," said Mrs. Stanton. "They haven't any letter on them."

"Those are all made at the oldest and the largest United States mint," said Mr. Stanton.

"That must be at Philadelphia," said Mrs. Stanton. "When I was a little girl, father took me through the old Philadelphia mint."

"You are right. That is *the* mint; and none of the money coined there has a special mark. That is why I wanted to get the silver money at Carson City. I thought I should be more likely to find the different mint marks. The teller at the bank looked over his silver, to help me, or I might not have found them all."

"I have been thinking about what kind of money they will give me in Washington," said Mrs. Stanton, "and I think I know."

Mr. Stanton shook his head. "I presume you do," he said, "but I don't want you to tell; for, in about two days, we shall reach Washington."

CHAPTER X

THE TREASURY IN WASHINGTON

"I WANT to see the White House," said Edith, as they drew near Washington.

"I'd rather see the Capitol," said Henry.

"I thought," said Richard, "that we were going to find out something about our money."

"So we are," said Mr. Stanton. "That's the thing we are specially interested in just now. We shall have to look at the other things as we do when we play that game of trying to see how much we can learn about things by just passing by them."

"I expect that I shall want to stop to look at the new station," said Mrs. Stanton.

"I suppose it is one of the most beautiful in the world," said Mr. Stanton; "it is certainly one of the largest. One of the best things about it is that it is so near some of the very buildings that we want to see."

"What buildings, father?" asked Henry.

"I'm going to see whether you can tell what they are, when you see them."

Half an hour later, when they reached the entrance of the beautiful station, Mr. Stanton said:

"Now, children, what do you see?"

"That big building with the dome and the statue on it must be the Capitol," said Henry. "It's too big to be anything else."

"What is the other building with the gold roof, father?" asked Richard. "I thought capitols always had gold domes."

"They often do," said his father; "but the Capitol hasn't one, and the building that you see is the Library of Congress."

"I see a tall monument, way over there," said Edith.

"That is the Washington Monument," said her father. "You can see that from any part of the city, because it is so tall. It's the tallest one in the world; and I think it ought to be, for the 'Father' of a country like ours deserves a tall monument. The Capitol is the first thing that we want to see, for that is where they make the laws about gold and silver money."

Though the Capitol seemed very near the station, they were several minutes in walking the distance. When, at last, they reached the great building, with long wings on either side, Mr. Stanton said:

"We can go in this door at the lower side."

"Please, father," said Edith, "I think it would be much nicer to walk up the front steps, as you do when you go to people's houses."

"That is just like you, Edith," said her father, putting out his hand to help her; "you always want to do the proper thing. I really think it does show more respect to the building."

When they reached the top of the long flight of steps, Mr. Stanton turned to the right side of the great stone portico and, pointing down, said:

"On this side is the place where Washington, when he was President, laid the corner stone of this building. Many noble men have stood where we are now standing, for this portico is the place where the Presidents are inaugurated."

"It's high, isn't it, father?" said Richard, when they entered the rotunda and looked up into the dome.

"It would take a good many boys like you, standing on top of each other's heads, to reach the top," said his father.

"Many as fifty, I should think," said Henry.

"Forty would be nearer, I think," said Mr. Stanton, looking in his guidebook, "if we were going to touch the inside roof; but we mustn't stop to figure that out now. I'm going to ask the guide to take us to the rooms where the laws are made."

"They sit behind desks, just as we do at school," said Henry, when they reached the Senate Chamber.

"If you look on each desk," said the guide, "you will find a little silver plate with the name of the senator who sits there."

"I hope," said Mr. Stanton, "that, some day, we can come to sit in the gallery, and hear them make the laws. There are a great many other things here, too, that we ought to see, so we shall certainly have to come again.

"Now, Edith, we will go down the steps that we came up."

"What a good place this is to see the Library of Congress!" said Mrs. Stanton, stopping on the portico. "Are we going over there? The children ought not to miss it."

"Just to see two or three things," answered Mr. Stanton. "Then we must hurry to the Treasury, or we shan't have time to go over it."

When they reached the Library, they stood a moment to watch the water of the bronze fountain, playing on the sea-nymphs and sea-horses, and even on the old god Neptune himself. Then they went up the steps and through the bronze doors till they came to the central hall.

"There is a great deal of gold inside the Library, as well as outside," said Mrs. Stanton, looking up at the ceiling.

"It isn't real gold, is it, father?" asked Richard.

"Yes; it is real gold, almost the very purest gold. Don't you remember that I told you, once, that gold can be hammered out very thin?"

"Yes, father."

"When it is rolled out so thin that it will just hold together, they call it gold leaf. When they want to make a ceiling like this, they put some sort of resin or glue on the wood, metal, or plaster, and then put the gold leaf over it. They use gold leaf, too, to gild the tops of books."

"It must cost a lot," said Henry.

"So it does; but even a grain of gold, when it is rolled out thin, will cover a good many square inches. Of course, the rain and the snow will wear the gold off the roof; but the gold inside here will last a long, long time. I don't wonder that they call gold 'the king of metals.'"

"I never saw anything so beautiful as this!" exclaimed Mrs. Stanton. "I don't want to hurry through these halls."

"But a glimpse of such beauty is better than nothing," said Mr. Stanton, "and, somehow or other, I keep thinking about New York and home."

"So do I," said Edith.

"A lunch room, in a library, seems rather strange," said Mrs. Stanton when they got off the elevator.

"Goody!" said Henry.

"I want you to sit at this particular table," said Mr. Stanton, drawing out the chairs.

"Oh, father!" exclaimed Richard. "Is that the Potomac?"

"That is the Potomac; and, if we went down the river, we should come to Washington's home at Mount Vernon."

"See there!" said Henry, pointing out a front window. "See the big statue of the woman on top of the Capitol."

"They call her 'armed Liberty,'" said his father. "She's a very tall woman, isn't she, and she wears a queer kind of a hat with an eagle and stars on it."

"Is there a real live eagle in Washington, father?" asked Edith.

"Nowhere except in the Zoo. The 'American Eagle' that we hear so much about is only a symbol, something like the flag. It means strength and power."

When they got off the car that took them to the Treasury, Mr. Stanton said:

"If we go around on this side, Edith can see the White House. It is just across the street, you see. Does it look as you thought it would, Edith?"

"I thought it would be taller," said Edith. "It looks something like that big house that we saw, last summer, out in the country, with the large lawn in front of it."

"I never saw a building like the Treasury," said Mrs. Stanton, as they turned around. "I should like to count the columns."

Just then, the children stopped almost in the middle of the walk, and their father and mother nearly stopped, too; for, coming out of the door of the Treasury, was a man in handsome uniform.

He wore gold epaulettes and a sword with a beautiful gold hilt; and there was gold on his hat, on his sleeves, and on his belt.

"We all forgot our manners, didn't we?" said Mrs. Stanton, as they went up the steps of the Treasury. "I never saw a handsomer uniform than that."

"I think he must be a general," said Mr. Stanton. "At any rate he had on a great deal of gold lace."

"I didn't see any lace," said Edith.

"That is what they call the trimming on uniforms," said her father. "It is made of gold thread. Just one grain of gold can be drawn out into yards and yards of fine wire. The gold workers take the wire, twist it around a fine thread, and weave it into bands, or use it to make fringes."

"There is a kind of cloth, called cloth of gold," said Mrs. Stanton. "When we get home, I'll take you to the museum, some day, and show you some gold brocades, such as the old queens used to wear."

"Here we are, at last," said Mr. Stanton, as they went into the Treasury. "We'll get a guide to show us around."

"Look, father," said Richard. "All the men here have brass buttons on their coats, and yellow stripes on their sleeves."

"These men have all been in the army, or in the navy," said his father. "A man that has loved his country well enough to fight for it, is just the man to guard his country's money."

The guard showed them a vault in the basement where he said more than a hundred million silver dollars were stored. Then he took them to another that contained both gold and silver money.

"See the paper money!" said Richard, when they came to

a room where sat some women, counting packages of bills so fast that it hardly seemed possible that they could tell what they were doing.

"They only finish making the paper money here," said their guide. "Most of the work on paper money is done at the bureau of engraving. The bills are brought here to be stamped with the seal of the government. That makes them money. It takes thirty days to make a bill."

"What becomes of the worn-out bills?" asked Mr. Stanton.

"They are cut up, then ground up, very fine, and made into board, such as book-binders use. You never know how much money may have been ground up to make the cover of your book."

"I thought we were going to have our money changed here," said Mrs. Stanton, who had noticed that Henry had his two-dollar bill in his hand.

"Change isn't just the word that we ought to use now," said Mr. Stanton. "We want to see what kind of money will redeem our bills. We will go to the cash room.

"We should like to have our bills redeemed, if you please," said Mr. Stanton, a moment later, to the cashier. "These boys want to learn what the United States keeps behind paper money."

When Mr. Stanton lifted Edith up, the cashier bowed and smiled. Then he took her dollar bill, put it in a drawer, and handed Edith a shining silver dollar.

"The bill you gave me isn't money now," he said, "because there isn't anything behind it. I have given you what stood behind it and made it money."

Then Henry handed the cashier his bill, and received one

silver dollar. Richard took his two silver dollars, and looked at them as though he didn't yet quite understand what had happened.

"I'll try a five," said Mr. Stanton, and in a moment he had five silver dollars in his hand.

When Mrs. Stanton stepped to the window with her twenty-dollar bill, Mr. Stanton said to the cashier: "Please give her as many different kinds of eagles as you can."

In a moment Mrs. Stanton turned around, and showed them a handful of gold money.

"Oh!" said Henry.

"Why didn't he give you gold, father?" asked Edith.

Richard didn't say anything, but looked quite disturbed over his two silver dollars.

"I knew, all the time, that he would give me gold, because my bill had a yellow back. That always means that it can be redeemed in gold."

"Let us see what you really have," said Mr. Stanton. "This large piece is an eagle; and this smaller one is a half-eagle; and these two little ones are quarter-eagles. If the cashier had given you one gold piece it would have been a double eagle."

"Show us the eagle," said Henry.

"Here he is," said his father, handing him the ten-dollar gold piece. "We've settled Richard's question, now; for we have found out that the United States keeps silver and gold behind all its paper money; and we have found, too, that paper money is made only in Washington."

"Then we use paper money, because it is easier to carry around, don't we?" asked Richard.

"Yes, my son. I'm glad you have thought that out. Now, what shall we do the rest of the afternoon?"

"I should like very much to go to the Zoo," said Edith.

"Well, little daughter, I think that, as the most of our trip has been for the boys, you ought to have your turn, so we will go to the Zoo. Just let me ask somebody a little about it. The Zoo is a large park, so we shall have to decide what we want to see."

"Eagles," said Edith.

"And bears," said Henry, "if they are in cages."

"We shouldn't any of us care to see them, if they were out of cages," said his father.

"Fortunately for us, the guide tells me that the bears and the eagles are at the same end of the park," said Mr. Stanton, hailing a car.

The ride was not a long one, and Edith soon had her desire, for they found a large cage of eagles, not far from the entrance to the Park.

"There are a good many kinds of eagles, aren't there?" said Mrs. Stanton. "Some of them are spotted, and some have crests. I think that one over in the corner must be a bald eagle."

"The eagle with the bright yellow on its bill, and the yellow feet is the war eagle," said Mr. Stanton. "Soldiers, way back in ancient times, loved to follow the standard of the eagle."

"See the peacocks!" said Richard. "I think they are prettier than the eagles."

"But they are proud," said his mother, "and neither the eagles nor the peacocks are so pretty as the swans down under that bridge."

The Hat Was Caught Between Two Rocks

"Let's stop to look at the swans," said Edith, as they went over the bridge.

"See that swan, Edith," said her father, leaning over the side of the bridge, and pointing down.

But, instead of the swan, Edith saw her father's hat falling into the creek below.

"Dear me!" said Mr. Stanton, putting his hand up to his head. "What shall I do without a hat!"

Before the others had time to realize what he was doing, Henry had run down the bank and had started out on the stones. Richard followed him, but hesitated when he looked at the stones. Richard could sometimes think faster than Henry; but, when it came to acting, Henry was much quicker, and Richard knew that.

Henry sprang quickly from one rock to another, and almost had the hat when the water suddenly carried it further away.

"Don't fall in, Henry!" shouted his father.

"I don't think he will," said Mrs. Stanton, quietly. "Henry is careful, as well as quick."

Over the stones went Henry again, and found that the hat was caught between two rocks just beyond his reach. He stopped a minute; then, looking at his umbrella, he took it by the top, reached out, and put the crook of the handle under the hat.

"He's got it!" shouted Richard.

So he had, and with a few more springs, and a run up the bank, he reached the bridge.

"Here's your hat, father!" he said, "and it's not very wet."

"I'm very much obliged to you, Henry," said his father. "There's no chance, in a zoological park, to buy a hat; and I certainly shouldn't look well, going around without one. I really must take back all that I have said about your umbrella. It has saved my hat, thanks to you."

Then they went up the hill to see the bears, and found cages filled with black bears, brown bears, and grizzly bears.

But Henry felt a little bit like a hero, just a little bit, but enough to make him lose his interest in bears.

So, after he had looked at them a moment, he said:

"I don't think bears are very good-looking animals."

"Neither do I," said his father. "Besides, it is time for us to go back to the station."

CHAPTER XI

GOLD AND SILVER MONEY

"I MUST say, boys," said their father, "that you have done very well, so far, in history; but, now that we are in sight of the mint, I'm going to tell you something that will probably surprise you. Before there was any United States, in what we call the early Colonial days, people didn't buy things as we do now. They paid for the things that they bought in corn or in cloth, or in codfish or even in bullets.

That wasn't a very easy way to buy small quantities of anything; for, if a man had only cloth to exchange, a small piece of cloth wouldn't do the other man much good. It is much more convenient, you see, to have one thing, like gold and silver money, that can be used to buy whatever a person wants to buy.

"When Washington was President, Congress established a United States mint, here in Philadelphia, and Washington gave some of his own silver, they say, to be melted up and made into money.

"Only a few years ago, the government built this new mint. Isn't it a handsome building?"

"This ceiling is gold, too," said Mrs. Stanton, as they went into the main hall of the mint. "I think it is almost as beautiful as the one in the Library of Congress."

"Only this one is what they call gold mosaic," said Mr. Stanton. "It is made of gold covered with glass; and, see, the mosaic pictures are pictures of children making money."

"There's one being a blacksmith," said Henry.

"There's a girl fixing a fire in a furnace," said Edith.

"And, there," said Richard, "is one weighing gold in scales."

"Here are some eagles, Edith," said her father, stopping on the stairs to look at two beautiful eagles, carved in stone, that stood, one on each side of the stairway, with wings outspread.

"We must hurry a little," said Mrs. Stanton. "Our guide is waiting for us."

"I am going to take you, first," said the guide, "to the marble corridor where you can look down to see how money is made. There," he said, pointing down, "is the melting room. In that room, all the gold and silver received, is melted."

"I'm rather surprised," said Mr. Stanton, "that you remelt the gold that comes from the assay offices."

"The work at the assay offices is well done," said the guide, "but, when the United States makes money, it starts at the very beginning, so as to be sure of every step. The honor of the government is represented by the money that it makes."

"Listen, children," said their father. "I like the word 'honor.' The government must maintain its honor, at any cost."

"Then, too," said the guide, "the pure gold and silver are

not hard enough to stand the wear of being used as money; so, in the melting room, they add a certain amount of copper."

"Isn't that a queer floor?" said Richard, pointing to the floor in the melting room.

"That iron grating," said the guide, "scrapes the boots of the men, as they walk over it. Every day, when the men are through work, the sections are lifted out, and the sweepings of the floor are put into a crucible, and there is always some gold melted out of the dust."

"I saw something, in a government report, about 'sweeps,'" said Mr. Stanton, "and I wondered what it meant."

"They save every particle of gold that it is possible to save," said the guide, "even to the ashes from the fires, the scrapings from the flues, the old gloves and aprons, and the settlings in the gutters on the roof. The government saves a good many thousand dollars just in saving 'sweeps.'

"That room is where the bars of metal are rolled out into strips so that the blanks for the pieces of money can be cut out.

Then, with big knives or shears, fastened in presses, they cut the long strips into short ones. They can cut ten gold or silver strips at a time.

"Down there they are cutting out the round blanks that are to be stamped. All the blanks have to be looked over, and the imperfect ones have to be melted up again.

"Then they weigh each blank; and, if it is not heavy enough, they send that back to be melted. If any are too heavy, they are filed down.

"After that they raise the edges of the coin—they call it 'upsetting'—so that it will not wear off too fast; then the coins are cleaned, and sent down to be stamped."

"That makes them into money," said Mr. Stanton.

"But that isn't the last thing that is done to the coin, before it is sent out as money," said the guide. "Last of all, after the coins are stamped, they are sent to a room where two women test every coin to see whether it rings true.

"They drop the coins, one after another, on a metal plate. If there is a hollow spot, or a bubble, inside, the coin won't ring true."

"I think I shall respect money more," said Mr. Stanton, "now that I know that it has to ring true."

"It has to weigh true, as well," said the guide. "Every piece of gold is weighed twenty times, before it goes out as money."

"Are they counting money on boards, in that room?" asked Mrs. Stanton.

"They count all the gold and the silver money by hand," said the guide, "but they count pennies and nickels on those boards, several thousand a minute. Even then, they have to work hard, especially just before Christmas, in order to supply the banks.

"One of our newest coins is the Lincoln penny. They are very pretty, for they are plated with gold. Perhaps you may like to get some, before you go, at the cashier's window.

"Here is the medal office; you may like to buy copies of some of the government medals. I especially like the one with Admiral Sampson's head. Those were struck after the Spanish-American War. There are medals in honor of other heroes; and there is always a new one for every new President.

"We generally leave our visitors here in the cabinet, where you will find many rare coins."

"It is clear to me," said Mr. Stanton, after the guide left

"Aren't They Beautiful?"

them, "that we could stay here all day without seeing everything; but we can't do that, so I'm going to look up some that the guide book specially mentions.

"Here is an old Greek coin with the date 700 B.C. Can either of you boys tell me how old that is?"

Henry put his hand up to his head, and twisted his face, because he tried so hard to think; but, after a minute, Richard said:

"Twenty-six hundred and ten years."

"That's right," said his father; "but I won't ask any more questions like that. We haven't the time."

"I've found the 'widow's mite,'" said Mrs. Stanton. "What does the guide book say about that?"

"That it is the smallest of the old bronze coins; and that it was found near the Temple in Jerusalem."

"It's just about as big as the end of a lead pencil," said Richard.

"There's one more that the children ought to see," said Mr. Stanton, "and that is one that dates back to the time of the Arabian Nights stories. Here it is. The old Caliph al Raschid himself is stamped upon it."

"Do you suppose it is like the ones that they used to do tricks with?" asked Henry.

"No; because this is only silver. You remember that Mr. Bailey said they used gold coins for the tricks."

"Is it beginning to be time for us to go home, father?" asked Edith.

"It's time for us to begin to think about it; but we can stay here a little longer. Let's go to the cashier's window and get some of the Lincoln pennies."

"Aren't they beautiful!" said Mrs. Stanton, as her husband gave each of them some of the shining coins.

"They certainly are," said Mr. Stanton. "There's one thing that I want you children to do; and that is, every time that you spend a Lincoln penny, I want you to stop and look at Lincoln's face."

"I think I shall begin a collection," said Richard, "and I'll begin with a Lincoln penny."

"The first money that the government coined was in pennies and half-pennies, so that is the best way to begin," said his father. "Now, I'm going to see whether I can get some Philippine money."

"Philippine money!" said Mrs. Stanton, looking at her husband in surprise.

"Yes, my dear; the Philippines belong to the United States. You coin money for the Philippines, don't you?" he asked, turning to the cashier.

"We make some of it here, sir," answered the cashier, "and of course we make all of the dies; but most of the work is done in San Francisco. There's more silver out that way, and then it is nearer the Philippines. The San Francisco mint has been busy, lately, turning Philippine money into United States money."

"Won't you tell us just what you mean by that?" asked Mr. Stanton.

"A lot of silver money, such as they used to use in the Philippines, has been sent over to San Francisco to be made into money bearing the stamp of the United States. They don't call their money by the same names that we do, but they have half-pennies and pennies, and so on, up to our dollar."

"The thing that I don't yet understand," said Mrs. Stanton, "is where the gold comes from that is made into ceilings and watches and all the other things that are made of gold."

"Many of the goldsmiths melt up money, and we sell some gold here," said the cashier; "but they do a good deal more of that business in the assay office in New York."

"So we have one right at home!" said Mrs. Stanton. "I really didn't know that."

"We'll go down to the waiting room, for a little while," said Mr. Stanton, seeing that Edith was very tired. "Then, little daughter, we'll go home by the fast express."

"I've got quite a collection now," said Richard, sitting down in a big chair in the waiting room, and taking a handful of coins out of his trousers pocket. "It's all Lincoln pennies and silver; but, anyway, I'd just as lief be a million silver dollar rich man, as a million gold dollar rich man."

"I wouldn't," said his mother, "unless I could get somebody to give me gold for my silver. I should want to go to Europe; and I know that when we were in Europe, one country wouldn't take another country's silver, but it would take gold."

"That's true," said Mr. Stanton. "What was behind our paper money, Richard?"

"Mother's had gold, and the rest had silver."

"But the gold," said his father, "is really behind the silver, for gold is the only money that one nation will take from another. Gold is the king of commerce, because it is the king of metals.

"Now, Henry, you've never told me what is behind coal and iron."

"I s'pose it's gold," said Henry. "Gold seems to be behind most everything."

"I think that our trip has been worth while," said his father, "if you have learned that the gold mines are what really keep all the business of the world going. That's why we couldn't have gone to California, if somebody hadn't been willing to work in a mine.

"But, Richard," said his mother, "if I had only gold, I couldn't buy little things, unless you let me have some of your silver money. They don't make even the gold dollars that they used to make. So we need the silver money and the nickels and the pennies."

"I rather think that mother has learned some things about money, don't you, boys?" said their father. "Now, I'm going to ask her a question; and we'll see whether or not she can answer it.

"Is gold a good king or a bad one?"

"That depends," answered Mrs. Stanton, quickly, "on the man behind the gold."

"You see, boys," said their father, "that there's really somebody behind the gold. Every man is king of his money; and a good man behind the gold, makes gold a good king."

"Father," said Edith, "isn't it most time to go?"

"Yes, we're going now. Start ahead, boys. This time, I'm not going to lose anybody."

"That's a beautiful doll!" exclaimed Edith, stopping in front of a shop window.

"We'll go in to get it," said her father, "while mother looks after the boys."

Richard and Henry, some distance ahead, were waiting for a chance to cross the street.

"Let's try, now," said Richard starting across.

Henry, seeing an automobile coming, drew back, and waited for the others to come.

While Richard was waiting for Henry, he saw a boy, not much larger than he, pushing a cart of peaches.

"Peaches, peaches, California peaches!" called the boy, cheerily.

"I wonder whether they really came from California," said Richard to himself. Then, seeing that Henry was still standing on the opposite corner, he added: "I've got time. I'll ask him."

Hurrying after the boy, who had just turned the corner, Richard said:

"Did they really come from California?"

"Sure!" answered the boy. "Want some?"

Before Richard could answer, a horse that had been standing at the curb took fright and plunged forward. The boy jumped, just in time to save himself; but the wagon lost a wheel, and the beautiful peaches went down into the street.

For an instant, the boy stood stupefied. Then turning to Richard, as if he felt that Richard could, somehow, help him, he said:

"I shan't have any money to take to mother tonight. What shall I do?"

Looking up the street, Richard saw Henry just coming across. Quick as a flash, he put his hand into his trousers pocket, pulled out a handful of coins, and thrust them at the boy.

"Take 'em," he said. "I've got to go!"

He looked so excited, and yet so pleased, that the others stopped, when they reached the corner.

"What has happened, Richard?" asked his mother.

Without answering, Richard put his hand into his pocket. When he pulled it out and opened it, they all saw, lying in his palm, a shining Lincoln penny.

"Got just that left," he said, smiling. "But that's enough to start a collection."

"What on earth are you talking about, Richard?" asked his father, sternly.

"Gave them to that fellow," he said, pointing down the street.

"When I get this family to the train," said his father, hurrying on, "I'll hear the rest of that story."

CHAPTER XII

HOME AGAIN

ON time to a minute," said Mr. Stanton. "I must say I'm glad to be back in New York. We have so many bags and bundles that you'll all have to carry something. We'll hope that somebody will meet us at the gate."

Up the long platform they went. Mrs. Stanton went ahead, carrying her big bag and an armful of wraps. Henry followed with his suitcase in one hand, and Edith's coat over his arm. Richard, carrying his suitcase, took hold of Edith's hand; and they kept as close as they could to their father. Mr. Stanton had a suitcase in one hand, and a big bag in the other; and, under his arm, he had a box with a doll that he had bought for Edith in Philadelphia.

"I wonder where Henry's umbrella is," said Mr. Stanton, glancing around.

"He left it in Philadelphia," said Edith. "He told me on the train. He feels pretty bad about it."

"Never mind," said her father, "we won't say anything about it. He really deserves a new one for saving my hat. Christmas will be here before very long, then we'll get him another."

When they reached the train gate, the children were very much surprised to find William, the chauffeur. Mr. Stanton wasn't surprised, for he had telegraphed to William to come; but he had a surprise, as well as the others, for there were grandfather and grandmother!

William took as many things as he could carry, and they followed him to the auto. Then William's brother took the checks; and, in a moment, off they went. William drove so fast that Mr. Stanton had to tell him, twice, that he was afraid the policemen would stop them. But no one did stop them, and there they were, at home!

John, the butler, came out to help them. Punch came out, too, barking as hard as he could, and jumped into the auto to find his little mistress.

In the hall they found Mary and Margaret waiting to help them off with their things; and, in just a little while they were all ready for dinner.

Mr. Stanton said that was the best dinner that Mary had ever cooked; and, though they had all talked so fast that they hardly knew what they had eaten, they all said that they were sure he was right.

Just as they were going into the library, the bell rang, and John came back with a telegram.

"Has business begun already?" said Mr. Stanton.

"I really do think," said Mrs. Stanton, "that they might have let you have one day."

"Oh!" said Mr. Stanton, "this is good news. Just listen:

"Ordered East. Just starting. Will wire you later.

"T. P. BAILEY."

They Followed Him Into The Auto

"I am glad," said Mrs. Stanton, "for I want, very much, to see Mr. Bailey."

Then they told grandfather and grandmother about Mr. Bailey; and Henry said that he wasn't sure whether he was going to be a prospector or a chemist. Then his father gave him Mr. Bailey's telegram, and he went over to sit by his mother in the window.

"I never used to think," said Mrs. Stanton, "that Central Park was very beautiful at this time of the year; but I must say that I had rather have our own park than the flowers they have in California."

Grandfather said he thought home always seemed a little better than any other place.

Grandmother, standing between Richard and his father, put her hand on Richard's shoulder, and said:

"I think Richard has grown tall."

"Perhaps he has," said his father. "I hadn't noticed it before. I do know, though, that he has been growing tall inside. Something I heard, just this afternoon, made me sure that he is growing unselfish."

Richard felt his cheeks grow red, and he had that queer, warm feeling around his heart. He was glad, just then, to hear grandfather calling him, and didn't wait to hear what grandmother said.

Grandmother did say something. She said:

"That's the best kind of growing."

Grandfather asked: "What are you going to be, Richard, when you grow up?"

"I don't know, yet," answered Richard; "but, when I'm anything, I'm going to be a collector, too."

That made funny little wrinkles come around the corners of grandfather's eyes; but he said he thought that would be a very good plan.

Then Richard showed grandfather his Lincoln penny; and grandfather told him that he had some of the large old-fashioned half-pennies and pennies that he would give him.

Grandmother said that she had something that she would give him; something that she had found, only a few days before, in one of her old pocketbooks; and that was twenty-five cents in paper money.

"I never heard of anything like that," said Richard.

"There were some in the cabinet collection in the mint," said his father. "I meant to show them to you. There were some little ten cent bills, and some for fifty cents."

"Those were very convenient," said grandfather, "and sometimes, when I want to send the children a little money, I wish we still had the old 'scrip,' as we used to call it; but, on the whole, I like the metal money better."

"But I don't like to think," said grandmother, "that, while we are sitting here, having a pleasant time, a lot of men are working down in the dark to get gold and silver to make money."

"I guess you don't know, grandmother," said Richard, "that the paper money has to have gold and silver behind it."

"I'll explain that to her, sometime," said grandfather. "Some men have to work down in the dark, and other men have to send their money into the dark, in order to keep the world going."

"What do you mean by that?" asked Mrs. Stanton.

"I mean," answered grandfather, "that there wouldn't be

any mines to work in, if men that have money didn't use it to open the mines. Nobody can be really sure how good a mine is going to be, so sometimes men lose all the money that they put into opening up a mine."

Grandfather was sitting by grandmother on the little sofa—he always sat by grandmother when he could—and, when he said that, she put out her hand and patted his hand gently.

Richard's father saw her do that; and he looked at grandfather, as if he wanted to ask him something.

Then grandfather said, "Yes, Richard"—he meant big Richard—"I lost some money that way, three years ago. We thought we wouldn't tell you; but perhaps it will help the boys to understand that the men in the light do help the men in the dark."

"Father," said Richard's father, quickly, "you must tell me, right away, if anything like that ever happens again."

Richard noticed that his father's voice was shaky, when he began to say that; but that it sounded real firm, before he got through, just as it sounded sometimes when he was telling the boys about things that they must do.

Grandfather must have noticed it, too, for he said right off:

"Yes, my son, I will."

Then they told grandfather and grandmother about the time that Richard was lost in the dark. Richard saw grandmother take out her handkerchief, so he went over and stood by her, and said:

"I'm here, grandmother, and I'm all right."

When Richard told grandfather how good the engineer was to him, grandfather said that all men, in the dark and in the light, were brothers and ought to help one another.

But Edith, in the big chair with her father, so quiet that he thought she must be asleep, was the one who had the last word. For, after grandfather said that men ought always to help one another, she sat up very straight, and the room was very still, and she said:

"Every night, just after I say, 'God bless everybody,' I'm going to say, 'God bless the miners.'"

www.ingramcontent.com/pod-product-compliance
Lightning Source LLC
Chambersburg PA
CBHW030611310726
48979CB00003B/664

* 9 7 8 1 7 6 1 5 3 5 3 5 2 *